One Thousand Years

RANDOLPH BECK

ISBN: 1490942890
ISBN-13: 978-1490942896

DEDICATION

In loving memory of my mother Marianne and my father John.

CONTENTS

CHAPTER ONE

"Up to a fairly recent date, the major events recorded in the history books probably happened.... Even as late as the last war it was possible for the Encyclopedia Britannica, for instance, to compile its articles on the various campaigns partly from German sources. Some of the facts — the casualty figures, for instance — were regarded as neutral and in substance accepted by everybody. No such thing would be possible now. A Nazi and a non-Nazi version of the present war would have no resemblance to one another, and which of them finally gets into the history books will be decided not by evidential methods but on the battlefield."

— *George Orwell, author and journalist, (February 4, 1944)*

Friday, February 4, 1944

It could never be certain whether one was dealing with racism or the simple bureaucratic inertia that every soldier must contend with.

"We were going at full throttle," First Lieutenant Sam McHenry explained. He understood the report was incredible but — as a black officer — white people had questioned his word too often. He had to wonder if a white officer would have as much trouble being believed.

"A P-40 can do well over three hundred miles per hour," he continued. "We were going just about that fast, and this thing just flew past us like a bullet."

Colonel Harriman scribbled some notes but didn't react. Captain Lawrence just sat there with his arms folded and had said very little. The British were often like that, McHenry thought. Stiff and proper, even while shivering in this drafty office that had only recently been an Italian farmhouse.

"Is it typical for you to use full power?" Harriman asked, with his precisely spoken British accent.

"No. It's not good for the engine. We had a call for emergency air support. A unit from the Eighth Army ran into some trouble and needed an assist."

"How was it none of your other pilots saw this?"

"It was too fast," McHenry swore. That was the question he had dreaded most. He relaxed a bit in the old wood chair and sighed. "I guess I was the only one looking up and to the right when it went by. Most of the other men did see it too, but only in the distance after it was almost gone. It was just a spec by the time they looked."

"You said you were heading northwest?"

"Yes, sir."

"And it was flying the same direction?" Harriman drilled.

"Almost five degrees more to the west," McHenry said. "I put the heading in my report."

"We want to hear it again, in your own words, as you recall it now," Lawrence said calmly. "This is a review, not an interrogation. Please tell us everything."

"This was right over Anzio?" Harriman continued.

"No, we were still fifteen minutes out. I don't even think we saw the shoreline yet."

"How accurate is this heading? Could it have been more like ten degrees?"

"No." McHenry looked over at the chart, and his eyes followed the direction indicated. "You're wondering if it could have been heading to Cassino, aren't you?" There was a battle going on there, McHenry knew, but he had not yet been part of it.

"Yes," said Harriman, casting a glance at the other British officer.

"Then the difference doesn't necessarily mean anything." McHenry looked back to the chart. "That's a long hop, and I would want to go there directly but that's not saying it's practical. Flying isn't like driving on a highway. A lot of these villages and fields look alike. We need to head to an initial position, a marker like a river or a distinctive building in the area to verify exactly where we are, and

2

then go from there. They would choose a spot that's behind their own lines, or one that's not contested. Nobody wants to get into combat while they're still trying to figure out where the front lines are."

"Interesting," Harriman said, contemplating the chart.

There was a pause, and then McHenry spoke. "Sir, may I ask about the fighting at Cassino?"

"Too soon to tell," Colonel Harriman replied briskly. It was probably a comforting lie. His face betrayed worry. Another pause, then: "It didn't take a shot at you?"

"Not that I'm aware of, sir. It just whizzed by."

Harriman slid a blank sheet of paper across the table. "Can you draw a picture of what you saw?"

"I've drawn half a dozen of these."

"Not for us."

"Lieutenant," Captain Lawrence began. "We are at the other end of the chain. By the time something gets to us, it has been transcribed, condensed and collated. No one I know has seen a picture from you."

"Understood," McHenry replied. Educated as an engineer, he pulled a pencil from the pocket of his flight jacket and started drawing. The aircraft was somewhat round, but it had a wedge shape at the rear. He had only caught a brief glimpse but it had been a clear day and the image was one he would never forget.

Lawrence unfolded his arms and leaned forward to see the lines McHenry was drawing. "No *Luftwaffe* insignia?" he asked, referring to Germany's air force.

"No markings at all," McHenry answered, still sketching.

"You say this was silver?"

"Shiny silver, almost like chrome."

"Outstanding," Harriman said. "I can already tell this is more detail than anyone else has seen yet."

"You mean this thing has been seen before?" That caught McHenry off guard.

"There haven't been very many," Lawrence said. "Just isolated reports. They are calling it 'night phenomena.' Some of you Yanks have reported a few as well. Yours is the first one seen in the daylight."

"No one really knows if they belong to the Boche," Harriman added. "The blighters have yet to fire a shot. This night phenomena is still just a curiosity, really. I guess now someone will have to contrive a new name."

Night phenomena. McHenry repeated the sound in his mind before returning to his sketch, giving more shape to the area beneath the round fuselage. He felt a little more at ease knowing that the two Brits didn't think he was crazy, but only a little. He mostly wondered if he would ever have to fight these things. The squadron was planning to transition to the P-39, and there were quiet rumors of moving to the P-47, or even the P-51, but he knew they would need more speed to take on this kind of aircraft. *A lot more.*

"The Boche are working on jets and rockets," Harriman said, as though sensing his apprehension. "But I have it on good authority that we're not too far behind them."

*

Captain Joseph Parker — call sign "Twain" — was waiting outside the farmhouse, which was a hastily arranged base of operations. McHenry observed how his own confident manner had eased the frown on his friend's face.

"It went well, Anthem?" Parker asked, referring to him by his call sign.

"Nothing to worry about," McHenry replied, briefly saluting. "These Brits have heard of these things before."

"Really? How can you call that 'nothing to worry about?' If it's real, there will be more."

Parker returned the salute and hopped into the jeep. They were two black men fighting in a white man's war. It would probably be the only salute Parker would receive until they neared the airfield of their own base. McHenry jumped into the passenger side and they drove off.

"I meant that they didn't think I was crazy," McHenry said.

"Did they tell you anything interesting?"

"Such as?"

"Rumors about the invasion. The fighting here in Italy will get easier when the Krauts have to fight it out on the French coast, too. Those Brits might have heard something."

"I didn't ask," McHenry said. "They didn't even want to talk when I asked about Cassino. I hardly think they would start babbling if I ask about the biggest secret of the war."

"Yeah, I guess not," Parker chuckled. He turned at the gate, and they crossed into a road through the Italian countryside.

"All they wanted to talk about was the mystery aircraft. It's not the first one reported, but nobody knows what it is."

"Ya know," Parker began. "This could be a sign of the end times."

"End of the war?"

"End of the war. The end of all wars. Judgment day."

McHenry turned his head to stare at the trees as they drove. "If you think so," he said. "But you know I don't. There's got to be a rational answer."

"You're the only pilot I know who doesn't believe in God," said Parker. "In fact, you're the only colored man I know who doesn't believe."

"Aw, come now, Twain," McHenry implored. "I don't know how many times I told you guys that I do believe in God. I just don't believe in church."

"Okay, okay. All I can say is you do need proper churching."

The jeep left the area and was on the open road. It was a long drive through Italian farm country. Narrow winding roads, distant farmhouses, and the occasional village would make the trip interesting as the sun started to descend. McHenry found it difficult to fathom that these people were just recently considered the enemy.

"There's one thing we have to consider," said Parker, briefly taking his eyes off the road to look up at the sky. "If that thing was German, and there's more than one, then that really is plenty to worry about."

"Yeah," McHenry sighed. "That's been bothering me a lot."

*

CHAPTER 2

"After the war...
We'll just press a button for food or for drink,
For washing the dishes or cleaning the sink.
We'll ride in a rocket instead of a car.
And life will be streamlined...
After the war."
— *Dorothy Roe, Associated Press, (March 20, 1944)*

Monday, March 20, 1944

Their starship was in sight.

SS-Sturmbannführer Kathy Dale was staring down into her SS side-panel when the pilot interrupted her.

"Docking in two minutes," he said. "You had better finish what you are doing with that game." He smiled at her, not for the first time this trip.

She looked up. The cigar-shaped starship was now clearly beside them, its pitch black webbing now filled nearly half of their 360 degree view.

"It's not a game," she coyly replied, the very slightest hint of a Chicago accent in her German. She smiled back at the blond pilot seated beside her. The forward, friendly demeanor was slightly out of protocol. *Leutnant* Adolf Vinson was a Luftwaffe man, after all, and she was an SS officer. It was her mission. He had been told only what needed to be done, but she knew the secret truths behind every deception — more of them anyway. The Luftwaffe wouldn't even be involved if they didn't need such a large starship to get here.

But his confidence had been infectious. He had promised a quick mission, and they had replaced the satellites in record time. And all the while he provided charming company. It was more than that, she understood. His Nordic features and idealist naivety reminded her of someone from her college years. That one had also been a younger man, and likewise an idealist. He actually wanted to marry her, an anti-social act that would put a serious dent into their positions with the campus Party leadership. She had planned to become a professor, after all, and a historian at that. *That*, she reminded herself, was a relationship best forgotten.

A new one with anyone like Vinson was impossible, or at least until the mission ends. She might go back to teaching then. But she can always dream in the meantime.

Vinson positioned the Tiger on a heading toward the hangar doors and released the controls to the machine. Everything would be automatic now.

"I hope we did not forget anything," he said.

"Like what?" she asked. It sounded like more small talk. She locked her side panel away and gazed at him. She would enjoy small talk for a while longer, knowing that she had a lot of work to do once back inside the ship.

They chatted a bit while the Tiger passed through the outer, and then the inner, hangar doors, and finally parking itself inside. It was a complex sequence handled automatically, but she could tell that Vinson was monitoring each phase, even as they laughed together. He was obviously born to fly. That was a trait he shared with those living in earlier times. She could well imagine Vinson as a pilot during the war they watched on the Earth below, shooting down Tommies, and defending the Reich. And she could be a simple schoolteacher in that much simpler time. Or they could be innocent students in a twentieth-century motorcar on their first date. She was an idealist, too, and she knew it.

Once parked, the engines shut down, the indicators turned blue and then disappeared. She regretted that Vinson had been so efficient, getting them back so quickly. Even in modern times, men had never lost their propensity for showing off.

Dale wondered how she could turn off her smile when they part ways. Finally, the view on the dome became a blank. The mission was really over. One indicator remained on, but only for a second longer. It was the mission log turning off. It would be retracted for analysis by the SS.

She knew that would happen, of course. What she hadn't considered was that no machines could be watching them now. They were suddenly truly alone. Anything they said would be erased before the next mission. This realization of privacy had startled her. Before this moment, she hadn't felt true privacy in years. For one brief second, she wanted to reach over and kiss Vinson good night. She resisted the impulse and laughed at the very idea.

Vinson laughed too, and she wondered if he understood the spirit of the moment.

"Thank you Adolf," she said. "I enjoyed the little trip." She squeezed his hand gently and it made her feel good.

*

CHAPTER 3

"The guy who goes around predicting Hitler will surrender tomorrow should have been up there today flying over that flak. The gunners are still in there pitching in the ninth inning."
— *Unknown airman, (April 8, 1944)*

Saturday, April 8, 1944

Sam McHenry had observed early on that war was like a series of engineering problems. It's not a single event, but a methodical process. Your own positions are fortified. The enemy's are torn down. Your side advances. One step at a time.

He could now see the target area more clearly. This was the best weather for dive bombing. It was fairly clear below, with some clouds above and around them. There was still quite a bit of haze in the west coming from Mount Vesuvius after the eruption last month. McHenry had noticed earlier that the birds were coming back.

"Target in sight," reported Parker, leading the mission of sixteen black fighter pilots that day. They were still flying their P-40s, but that was due to change this month.

McHenry looked ahead to Brooks' aircraft, who would be up next, and then swept his eyes left to locate the small dot that was Parker, now making his dive. He didn't hold his eyes there long. They darted back and forth, scanning the horizon, even turning his head both ways for a full view, and then to his gauges and instruments. He switched fuel tanks in preparation for the dive, and scanned the horizon again.

"Taking some flak," shouted Parker over the noise. "It's coming from one..." The reception broke for a moment of crackle, then came back. "...away." Parker had dropped his load and pulled up, and to the side.

Brooks was now starting his dive, and the flak would soon be aimed at him.

McHenry checked his gauges again, and then the bomb-safety lever. The aircraft was running smoothly. Scanning outside, he looked down to see Parker's bomb explode at the bridge. It looked good, but he was too far away to make a real assessment.

"Good shooting, Twain," said Brooks, taking his turn to shout over the flak. "Close, but the bridge is still up. I'm almost there." Another pause, and he released. "Bomb away," he said.

McHenry lowered his flaps and began his own dive, heading downward at sixty-five degrees. The flak was directed at him now. After dozens of missions like this, he felt that knew the Germans' playbook. The temptation to defend himself was great. He wanted so badly to reciprocate with his .50 cals, but he had to concentrate on that bridge. His ears cleared, and so did his mind.

"Bridge still up, but smoking," he shouted, reporting on Brooks' hit. He stayed quiet from then on, wanting to be completely focused for the last moment before releasing his bomb.

That moment was approaching as though in slow motion. His cockpit shook hard as the enemy's flak exploded around him. He made an instantaneous decision to fall another three seconds — a long and dangerous three seconds — to get the aim right. Then he released the bomb and pulled up, pushing the throttle, feeling the intense gee-forces, and resisting the unrealistic fear that the wings could snap off, or the very real worry that those gee-forces could force him to black out.

But that worry was short-lived. He was okay, and his plane was okay. It felt good to be rid of the 1,000 pound bomb that was dragging him. He gained altitude quickly to rejoin the group in a circle around the target, while checking for damage from that flak. There must have been damage, he knew, but he couldn't see any of significance. His eyes scanned the sky again, hoping for a repeat of their recent air battle. He wondered, too, about that remarkable silver ship he'd seen those months before.

The next man dropped his bomb, increasing the damage to where it could not be easily repaired. But then Douglas sighted enemy aircraft above. Coming from a dive, the German fighters would be quickly on them.

Parker turned hard right, leading them into the attack. "Battle stations, people! Those still carrying, find a good place to jettison, but get in formation quick!"

"'190s," Brooks shouted — meaning the Focke-Wulf 190, the Luftwaffe's versatile fighter. They had tangled with '190s before. The Germans were faster, and could climb higher, but the P-40 was more agile and had better armoring. Today, the Germans' main advantage was their numbers. There were simply more of them this day. *Too many more.*

"I count at least twenty," said Rebbit, one of the new replacements.

"At least," agreed Parker. The formation tightened up. Parker saw that the enemy aircraft were going to overcast — coming in too high. He made a sharp right, leading the men under the Germans.

Now the real fighting would begin. They broke off into pairs, McHenry with Douglas, as the '190s did as well. But the numbers quickly made coordination impossible.

McHenry was attempting to line up on a '190, only to find another attacking from behind him. He turned, trying to shake him loose, but the man stayed on him. He cut his power and turned into a tight barrel roll, letting his follower overtake him. That worked. Then he pushed the throttle to stay close behind. He almost had it in his sights but a second '190 came from the side, now firing at him. McHenry made a wild corkscrew turn, coming out of it nearly lined up on the second '190. They both turned and banked, but McHenry was turning tighter, reaching for the sweet spot where their swerves could cross the trajectory of his shells. Finally, he pushed the trigger.

He expected to see his tracers spit forward but they didn't. His guns didn't fire. He pushed the trigger again, with no result. With another '190 behind him, he jinked left so hard it was difficult to get his fingers to check the gun switches. They were already on. He reset them quickly, to no avail. Leveling off only long enough to clear his mind and try it again, slowly, his guns still didn't fire. He toggled the gun switches off and on one more time. Nothing.

"My guns are out!" he called. "Repeat, this is Anthem; my guns are out."

Douglas was quick to reply. "Jammed?"

"Negative. Appears electrical."

"Reset your gun switches," Douglas said, sounding out of breath. They were all busy.

"Tried that," McHenry said, making another tight turn while looking back and forth for the '190s he was tangling with, and then deciding to dive toward the trees. He couldn't blame Douglas for the obvious suggestion. Allowances are made for the stress of combat. He'd have suggested that, too.

"Anthem, Twain," Parker called. "Having trouble spotting you. Can you get home?"

"West of the main," McHenry replied, seeing the '190 on his tail again. Then he saw there were two of them again, and immediately took this as an opportunity to help the others win the day. "Leading two away on a chase. Don't worry about me; will shake these guys." No sooner had he said that that he saw one more with them. *Even better*, he thought. *This could help even the odds for the rest.*

He hugged the contour of the ground, hills and valleys, nearly clipping the trees. He had to keep looking behind, then forward, occasionally seeing the Germans' tracers fly by, and occasionally missing trees and high tension wires by inches. He went as fast as he could while jinking. At 275 miles per hour, he was as likely to be killed by a tree as by the Germans.

He tried aiming toward the direction of his base but the three '190s had the advantage. His heading was determined more by their attacks than by his own intent. The best he could do was jink out of their sights while they seemed to control the general direction. He didn't mind at first, as long as it wasn't north. He was still alive. Then they reached the end of the landscape, and they were out skimming over the sea.

"I'm out over the water," he reported, although certain the men were out of range by now, especially at this low altitude. He kept jinking left and right, up and down, and picking up salt spray. The Germans rarely had a good shot at him. One of them was gone now, probably back to rejoin the fray, but possibly out of ammunition. Bullets are heavy. An aircraft can only carry so many. It gave him hope that they might run out, too. The other two kept at him, and they scored more hits. Seeing that he was leaking fuel, he changed tanks so that he could empty that one first. There was still enough hope that he was able to think ahead.

The nose kept veering right. In a quick glance, he saw the edge of his starboard wing now torn up. But, thankfully, his controls still responded. He needed them. His life depended on his maneuverability. He kept up his jinking, but they still forced him out further over the sea. They scored more hits, one rattling the armoring at his back. Wind hissed through a new misalignment of the airframe, but the aircraft held together. Then the controls became sluggish. He didn't even need to look behind him to know that most of his rudder was shot out — a death sentence, he knew.

Ditching would be the smart thing to do. One of these Germans still gets credit for a kill, and he wouldn't need to die. Would they let him live long enough for that? *It didn't matter*, McHenry resolved. He was never going to give in. *Never*. He pulled the yoke hard. The plane could still respond well up and down, so he kept at it, jinking vertically. He only needed to last long enough for them to run out of bullets or fuel.

Then the two remaining '190s were gone. He'd have expected them to climb first, but they turned eastward, rising only slowly to a less crazy altitude, and clearly favoring maximum speed. Then he saw what made them run off.

"Anthem!" a voice shouted. It was Parker, having made a beeline from the target area. Two planes were up at five hundred feet.

"You're just in time," McHenry said. "I was just about to put them all into the Tyrrhenian Sea." He rose steadily, angling to join them, and then saw another formation of planes coming at them. It was the rest of the mission.

"You know," Douglas laughed, "we saw you kept dodging 'em even after they'd gone."

"Better one too many dodges than one too few," he replied dryly. He counted fifteen planes above him. They didn't lose anyone. Only then did he check his gauges and decide to switch fuel tanks again.

"We were afraid you..." Parker started.

Twack! McHenry's plane shuddered hard when a bird struck his nose. The impact rattled the cockpit, loosening a battered wiring harness. His engine lost power. His prop was windmilling.

"My engine's out," he said, dropping away. He understood that his radio must also be out, but followed up as a matter of procedure. "Anyone read me?"

No one replied. He could see Parker breaking off, and the other men reforming. He took a deep breath and saw this for another point where he would have to define himself. He'd either make it or die right here and — either way — he was going to do it like a man. He played with the yoke to test the controls, and scanned the horizon for land. At well under four hundred feet, there weren't many options other than to glide back toward land. He began turning in that direction as smoothly as his damaged rudder could handle.

"I've got control," he said, lowering his flaps. He turned off his useless gun switches, and tried restarting the engine. When that failed, as he knew it would, he recycled the battery and generator switches, and then the circuit breakers. He was indeed going down. Every retry of the engine was simply going through the motions. He slid open the canopy and felt the sharp breeze on his face. This was real to him now.

Parker pulled up, engine cut and flaps down, to pace him on his descent, sliding open his own canopy. He made a *follow-me* motion with his arm, and then turned right — away from land.

McHenry followed without questioning, and saw. There was a Navy warship only a few miles away. He gave his friend a thumbs-up gesture. He knew that one of the men would be on the radio, telling them to prepare to retrieve him. Indeed, as they passed under 200 feet, the ship was already beginning its turn. They would be coming for him. The other men in the squadron circled above, marking the spot.

He could taste the salt spray in the air, and knew that Parker should have leveled off long before now. The end was coming. He wanted so much to say what a pleasure it was flying with them all. But there was no time left. He saluted crisply.

Parker returned the salute, clearly saying words that McHenry could read on his lips, *"Godspeed, Anthem."*

Already dangerously low, Parker powered up to begin leveling off, watching him continue his descent. The end was coming. McHenry pulled back and flared in the last seconds.

The plane touched the water and skipped nimbly once, allowing McHenry one final moment of free flight, then slammed hard into a cresting wave. He was struck unconscious immediately, still strapped to his seat. Parker was calling to his dead radio, pleading for him to awake and get out of the sinking plane.

He couldn't hear the calls; he couldn't even hear the planes flying overhead or the sound of the waves splashing against the broken canopy. The blood dripped from his ears as the cockpit filled with cold seawater, the engine's weight pulling it down. His fellow airmen would still be circling when the ship arrived. But the spot they marked was just an oil slick on the water now. His plane was on its final approach to the bottom of the Tyrrhenian Sea.

To a man, each whispered a tearful prayer for Sam "Anthem" McHenry, Lieutenant, United States Army Air Force.

*

Dale looked on as Vinson maneuvered them beside the sinking warplane. Submerged, they moved slowly under the water. Although passive sensors were limited here, the system gave the illusion of clarity up to the distant shore.

"Watch out for that approaching ship," she warned. "It will be overhead in five minutes."

"Not a problem," he answered, grinning confidently. "We will get this one." He slowed their pace again as their Tiger neared the destination.

She smiled back. His confidence was infectious.

And why shouldn't it be? Others from the starship had twice tried to recover twentieth-century men, but they failed each time. Operational parameters required caution in such abundant quantities that failure was almost guaranteed. Yet, they were so close now it seemed as though nothing could go wrong.

"We are there!" said Vinson excitedly.

Dale sent the grappler after the primitive airplane fuselage, stopping it from sinking further. Now she just needed to extract the American. A second arm tore away the canopy, and then cut the seat belts.

"It goes well," said Vinson.

"Do not say that yet," she said, pulling the near-lifeless body toward the medical container in the small cargo bay. The main grappler released the airplane and pulled back inside.

"No!" she sighed. The arm was too large and unwieldy to manipulate the container. She stifled a derogatory comment about the lack of more suitable equipment. With years for careful planning, they should not have needed to rely on the Luftwaffe.

"They are designed for heavy work under combat conditions," Vinson explained.

She tried to ignore him, focusing her attention on the task and making several more attempts to transfer the unconscious man into the container that could preserve his life. "He's dying out there!" she gasped.

Vinson released the restraint on his seat and snapped up. "How much time is there?"

"Maybe two minutes."

"We are deep enough to avoid that ship. You can still take us deeper if you feel the need to."

"You can't go out there" she said, incredulous.

"I have my emergency pack," he reminded her, holding one hand on the harness strapped across his chest. "I will not put the mission at risk but you may activate it if I do."

He stepped toward the door without waiting for a response, but then turned once more. "I really mean that. Do not feel any guilt if you need to do this." And then he ran out of the cockpit, disappearing from view.

Dale turned back toward the front end of the dome and cursed herself for not being more assertive. She held the authority, after all. Besides that, he was only a *Leutnant* in the Luftwaffe. She was a *Sturmbannführer* in the SS. Then she looked at the rapidly fading life signs for the American, and was a little bit glad that Vinson could be so reckless.

Was he really going to swim out there? she wondered. Her familiarity with the Tiger was rudimentary at best. She had been trained to fly them in an emergency, but the workings of the small airlock underwater was a different matter. She didn't know how long it would take to cycle and they were definitely running out of time.

Then there was the question of the emergency pack Vinson wore, an awkward term for a personal self-destruct device. They were very efficient, and she was certain it could do the job even underwater. Vinson would be killed, his body dissolved in milliseconds. There was no doubt in her mind that she would indeed activate it if necessary, and that she would feel no guilt, only regretful sadness. They were in the twentieth-century. History was something she understood only too well. She would do anything to protect it. That's why she was here.

The seconds would tick by slowly before she saw the hatch open. Vinson's head popped out. She was surprised to see he wore no spacesuit. He climbed toward the American's body, crawling along the mechanical arm, careful to avoid the hazardous materials surrounding the ship. He worked like a man who knew what he was doing, but she reminded herself of the dangers. Those dangers were not just to Vinson alone. Were he to introduce some kind of change into the present, the change could be magnified through time. This would affect the *Führer*, the Reich and all mankind. She watched the indicators on her SS side-panel, reminding herself that she knew what she was doing, too. Everything was still safe. She worried anyway. That was her job at this moment.

Vinson had moved the American's inert body into place, gingerly but firmly. The capsule closed immediately, and he rushed back toward the airlock. It was then that she realized she had been holding her breath all this time until the hatch had sealed.

She guided the Tiger to a safe distance. Her side-panel showed the American's body being put into the resuscitating phase of its program. The man would recover. The capsule will keep him alive until a medical officer revives him.

"He's going to make it," she said as Vinson entered. His uniform had dried itself quickly, such was the material of the modern Third Reich, but his face and hair were still wet. And his nose was bleeding. She guessed the quick change of pressure to be painful, but he was still grinning.

"I'd better get the medical kit," she said, grinning back. "You came out too fast. Maybe I should have increased the cabin pressure."

"No," he said. "I could have waited in the airlock. I wanted to see how he is doing."

"You got him in time." She wanted to be mad at Vinson, but couldn't. He was willing to give his life for the Reich, the mission, and for someone he didn't even know. That was worth something.

She thought about the moment that would arrive later, when the records were ejected, and the recording was off. She knew better than to imagine giving him that kiss. Perhaps another squeeze of the hand would suffice until that day when they finally return to their own time.

*

CHAPTER 4

"On this morning of hope we may speak of our firm conviction. We may hope because we are strong, because we believe. Our hope is in the victory and freedom of the Fatherland, in the message of our sword."
— *Nazi Party message on Easter morning,*
(April 9, 1944)

Sunday, April 9, 1944

McHenry's eyes fluttered open and looked up in the bright light. His mind was still in mid-dream, but he sensed that this light was different from the one in the other dream. It was a harsh light and he didn't like it.

He heard a man's voice. It was in German.

Another man stepped over to the equipment encasing McHenry's body and peered down into his patient's eyes. The man said something in German to the young officer standing beside him. He took a quick glance at the charts on the large screen behind the patient, as though to confirm his reasoning. McHenry was dazed but coming around. "Do not be alarmed," the second said, in English with only a slight German accent. "You are still healing but you will be fine. Breathe deep."

McHenry was groggy and slow, yet alert enough to guess from the white tunic that the young-looking man hovering above him was a doctor. "Where?" he stammered. The word from his lips had somehow startled him — as though another part of his brain was surprised to hear himself talk.

"You must breathe deep," the doctor insisted. McHenry took the deep breath and some of the fog lifted. The doctor could see the results on a panel. "That is good. Take two more deep breaths."

McHenry couldn't remember where he was last, or how he got here, but he knew this wasn't a good place to be. He was thinking more clearly now. His worst suspicions were quickly confirmed when he saw the crooked cross of a swastika on the man's collar. He took another deep breath and turned his head to examine the other man.

The doctor appeared youthful, tall and muscular, but the blond-headed first man looked even more like a picture straight out of Nazi propaganda imagery. He wore a light blue uniform. It wasn't exactly like the Luftwaffe uniforms McHenry had seen black-and-white photos of, but there were pilot wings on the man's lapel and, of course, the swastika emblem on a button below his collar.

A third man stepped into view. It was a black man in a black SS uniform, armband and all — or something like an armband. McHenry took another deep breath. *A black Nazi!* That didn't make any sense. He decided it must be part of a dream. The black man said nothing although he must have known his presence frustrated McHenry's comprehension.

The junior Luftwaffe officer took the initiative. "You are on a ship," he said gently. He paused and looked at the doctor as though looking for his approval. "It will not be easy for you to accept this but you can consider us to be your friends. The doctor tells me that you still have some healing to do. I promise you it will be fast. You must lie still for a few minutes longer."

McHenry took another deep breath and felt much better. He was becoming fully alert. The black Nazi reminded him of Mike Jenkins, a student at Tuskegee. Jenkins was sharp and had been training with them for a few weeks until the Army decided he was just too big to be a pilot. But these men were even bigger than Jenkins. A lot bigger.

He looked down and saw the metal box that enclosed his torso. There was also a metal band strapped to one arm, and something on his head, which he thought might be bandages of some sort. He couldn't see his legs from the other side of the equipment but they felt free. He stretched his legs as he looked around to examine the room. This was a large room with two other beds like the one he was lying on. Each bed had a large white panel on the wall behind it. He tilted his neck back to look at the panel over his own bed, which wasn't blank at all. It was brightly lit with lists of numbers and some German writing in one corner, but most of the panel displayed what looked like a brightly colored cartoon image of the inside of a human body. His body? He stretched his free arm and the image on the screen moved accordingly. Curiously, some of the numbers changed as well.

McHenry wondered if this could be an elaborate ruse intended to coerce secrets out of him. The uniforms just seemed a little different from the photos he had seen. Or they might be homemade renditions for someone's strange idea of amusement. He looked back at the medical screen behind him, and raised his arm again. Even the best white hospitals didn't have this kind of equipment. Without waiting for an answer, McHenry tried lifting himself out of the contraption but quickly gave up struggling. He was firmly attached to the device.

"Who are you?" he finally asked, staring at the black Nazi. The words came out easily this time.

"You have been through much," the doctor said. "You suffered from drowning, some broken bones, including your skull. The treatments you received have been successful and we will be able to remove the equipment in a few minutes. I am *Doktor Oberleutnant* Evers. This is *Oberführer* Mtubo; and here is *Leutnant* Vinson. Herr Vinson was one of the people who rescued you from sea."

"Well, thanks," McHenry acknowledged sarcastically. He couldn't feel that anything was broken. He still didn't remember crashing but that, at least, sounded plausible. More plausible than a black Nazi, anyway. He thought through his briefings, trying to remember Nazi ranks, and guessed an *Oberführer* to be something like the Nazi equivalent of a colonel.

Oberführer Mtubo stepped to the side of the bed and stood with his hands behind his back, looking down his nose at McHenry. It was a smug pose, as smug as he would expect from any Nazi in the movies. "This might have been easier for you if I had waited until you were fully recovered. Even so, your mind would still find this difficult to grasp. Simply put, we have come here from your future."

"You're saying that you're time travelers?" McHenry asked warily.

"I mean exactly that," said Mtubo. "We went backward through time. We left our home in the year 2968."

McHenry said nothing, unsure which was easier to believe, time travel or a black Nazi or the whole notion of a black officer seemingly in charge of these other men. The black Nazi didn't even look old enough for the rank he appeared to hold.

"Consider it this way: The aircraft of your day were not possible fifty years ago. Yet even now the Reich is building weapons that will smash London from the coast of France. Mere decades from now, they will build rockets that can fly to the moon."

The American still did not answer, so Mtubo went on. "Do not be surprised what can be possible after one thousand years. This ship can travel through time just as your primitive aircraft can fly through the air."

McHenry raised his head slightly. "Does that mean we lost the war?" He knew it was a stupid question, but he needed to be sure.

Mtubo laughed, none-too-gently. "The Reich prevailed, just as it always has and always will."

McHenry pushed his head back into the restraint and let out a sigh.

"From our point of view, the war you were fighting ended long ago," Mtubo continued. "You may consider yourself to be our guest here, Lieutenant. The *Kommandant* of this ship may even grant you some limited privileges to walk about the ship, but do not attempt to interfere with our operations here."

The *Oberführer* did not wait for a response. He turned to Vinson and spoke in German, issuing an order McHenry couldn't hope to understand.

"*Jawohl!*" Vinson replied with a click of his heels.

"*Heil Renard!*" Mtubo said, thus ending the conversation.

Vinson and the doctor clicked their heels against the deck and echoed the *Oberführer's* salute. "*Heil Renard!*"

Mtubo turned and strode out the door, which seemed to slide open without prompting. The door closed behind him on its own.

McHenry lay there, pulse-pounding, dumbfounded. He had understood only the *Heil* part. "I'm guessing Renard is your *Führer* now," he finally said.

"Yes, she is," the doctor answered.

"She? You mean, your *Führer* is a woman?" He resisted the urge to laugh.

"Yes." The doctor was looking directly at him now to see his reaction.

"Ah!" McHenry said. It all made a kind of sense. Then he laughed. "It's nice to know you're not heiling Hitler anymore."

"You have seen Adolf Hitler only through American propaganda," said Vinson, obviously a little offended at the remark.

"*Leutnant*," the doctor said to Vinson, "there will be plenty of time to talk about such matters when Herr McHenry has become fully acquainted with his situation. He needs time."

"No," McHenry protested. "I can talk about this right now."

Vinson sighed. "Dr. Evers is correct. I have to return to my debrief. There will be time for us to talk later. I hope we can become good friends." He held out his large hand for McHenry, who accepted the handshake only with suspicion. "I will see you later today if it is all right with the doctor."

"That should be fine," the doctor said.

McHenry watched as the automatic door opened for Vinson. Mtubo was right about one thing, he realized. His predicament was hard to accept. All of it. It was easier to believe that these men were from the future than that America had lost the war. *We were doing so well*, he thought.

But as the door closed behind Vinson, McHenry understood there could be no better explanation. These men were indeed from the future. And Germany had won the war. He was probably safe enough for now. The only important question was, will he ever see home again? Then he saw the swastika on the doctor's tunic again. No, he realized. The first question was, how was he going to escape?

"We can only imagine what you are going through," Dr. Evers said. "If it is of any consolation, please know that there has been a lot of concern throughout the ship for your well-being."

"Thanks," McHenry replied stiffly.

CHAPTER 5

"If Fascism comes to America, we shall not even have the excuse of being the first fooled."
— John Land, The American Mercury, (April 1944)

"All is finished. You are ready to be removed from the machine," Dr. Evers said, keeping his eyes on the images. He stepped back as the enclosure slid down from around him. In three seconds, it seemed to McHenry that they just dissolved into the frame of the bed.

Naked, McHenry sat up and looked down. There were no scars. He felt like a new man. "Do you have my clothes?"

The doctor spoke in German to no one in particular, something he called *Rechner*, and a drawer opened at the wall. It revealed a neatly folded sky blue uniform with a pair of boots. Taken aback, and ever distrustful of his benevolent captors, McHenry grabbed the whole ensemble and placed them in a pile on the bed. The drawer closed again, leaving him to wonder whether it would have closed immediately had he not taken it away. He was going to comment about the rechner but he chose not to. If this truly was the future, he could assume the Hollerith machines would have improved beyond the relays and punch cards of his day.

The garment's material was strange, but of plain design. The pants pulled up loosely, with no belt or zipper, as though they were several sizes too large. But the fabric tightened up once it reached his waist. Almost like magic, they became a perfect fit.

"Whoa!" he said aloud, and then cursed himself silently for revealing his surprise.

"I had not expected that our clothing would surprise you," said the doctor. "But I should have. Technology has advanced immeasurably in even these minor details."

McHenry didn't need the doctor to tell him that. He pulled the blue shirt over his head, and it tightened up around him in a way that

25

seemed almost alive. He stood erect and looked down at himself. This was most definitely a Luftwaffe uniform, much like Vinson had worn, but it had no markings on it, and thankfully, he thought, no swastikas.

"These boots are the most comfortable I ever had," he said finally.

"The analysts who went through your effects had commented on the primitive nature of your clothing. You will certainly find life to be very comfortable in our time. Would you like some coffee?"

"Yeah, sure." McHenry followed the doctor to a small office adjacent to the infirmary. This could be a good time to make a break for it, he thought. He sized up the doctor, who was a foot taller and clearly quite brawny. Then he remembered that Vinson and Mtubo were the same height. If all the men on this ship were this big, it would be difficult to find circumstances where he could take any one of them on. The office door closed behind them, automatically like the others. McHenry would have to learn what made them open and close before he could entertain any notion of escape.

The doctor sat behind a desk and gestured for McHenry to take a seat beside a wall covered with anatomical illustrations. "Cream or sugar?"

"Yes, both please."

The doctor said something in German — a command for the rechner — and a slot beside the doctor's desk opened with two mugs of steaming coffee. The swiftness astounded McHenry, who couldn't imagine that coffee could even be poured in the time this took, let alone brewed.

The doctor gave one of the cups to McHenry. "You will learn to appreciate the technology we have here, Lieutenant."

McHenry tasted the earthy brew and was pleased. "Your rechner makes good coffee." He liked the doctor but fought the temptation to reply more respectfully than propriety demanded.

"This ship has the best of everything. You are on the finest ship in the Reich." But the doctor may have sensed he should not rush the man into appreciating what to him had only recently been an enemy nation. It was a difference probably greater than the thousand years time.

"You can say you were resurrected on Easter Sunday," the doctor joked.

"That's blasphemy, Doctor," McHenry responded.

"Are you a religious man?"

"I wasn't before today. I'll have to see how the day goes. Regardless, I am respectful of others."

"It is a good way to be," the doctor said contritely. "You have my apologies. Well, then, you must have many questions."

"Yes," McHenry answered without hesitation. "How many Negro Nazis are there?"

The doctor didn't even try hiding his smile. "The world has changed since your times. People have changed. It is only natural that the Reich would change, too."

"It can't be that simple."

"Yes, it can. We have had one thousand years of social progress. The nations of the world, as you knew them, have all joined the Reich long before I was born. The people are so much more interdependent in modern society."

McHenry wasn't ready to believe. It was too much to hope for, too much to believe. He had heard too many promises in the past. But he wasn't going to argue over it either. It was better to get back to business.

"Well, what happens to me now? When can I go home?"

The doctor sat back, held his breath for a moment and exhaled visibly. "I am afraid you can never go home." He paused for another moment as the meaning of this answer could sink in.

McHenry was not surprised but would pursue any argument. He would grasp at any straws if need be. "I am entitled to the rights of a prisoner of war under the Geneva Convention with all the privileges of my rank. You are required to contact the Red Cross to notify them of my capture."

"You know that is impossible. You are not a prisoner. You are a guest. That war is over for all of us." The doctor leaned forward again, but looked into his coffee. "History records that your aircraft was lost over the sea, and your body was never recovered. If you

27

were to return to your home in the present day, your actions would affect how events were to unfold. Even if you only introduced one small change into history, that one change could ripple through an entire chain of events, causing some of our people — perhaps even my grandparents — to never have been born."

McHenry mulled that over, looking for a way out. "But then couldn't your picking me up change what happens?"

"In theory, yes. You are taking in the complexities of time travel very well. There are still some theoretical risks but there was no chance that you could affect history. We had taken all possible precautions. Your aircraft was already underwater. You were deep enough that our equipment needed to clear your airway and restart your heart."

"And I suppose that's easy to do nowadays." McHenry looked again at the diagrams on the wall.

"Very easy to do, if we can recover you in time. Your bones were already repaired even before your body came aboard this ship. My greatest concern was that brain damage would cause loss of memory."

McHenry sighed. That might have been for the best, he thought. Then he took another sip of coffee and remembered night phenomena. Were they from the future too? "Tell me, Doctor. We had seen a very fast aircraft. Could that have been you guys?"

"Absolutely not. We had taken great pains to ensure that no one would see us. You probably saw some of the jets or rockets the old Luftwaffe developed during that war."

A chime sounded, prompting the doctor to tap the swastika button on his collar. "Evers," he said.

A woman's voice spoke. McHenry recognized only the word "*Amerikaner*" and assumed that was about him. He was startled that a woman was aboard the ship, but kept this thought to himself.

"*Jawohl!*" replied Dr. Evers. He released the button and stood. "The *Kommandant* is ready to see you now. Are you ready to see more of the ship?"

"Certainly," McHenry said. He stood and took one more sip of his coffee. It had not cooled off in the slightest. "One more thing, Doctor. What if we had seen your ship; would that change anything?"

"It might have ramifications," the doctor conceded. "But do not build up false hopes. We know what we are doing. We have been very meticulous in our work."

The doors opened for them as Dr. Evers led the way out of his office, through the familiar dispensary and out into a long wide corridor. There were, indeed, women aboard the ship. They passed several men and women wearing Luftwaffe blue or SS black. All were tall and fit like the others McHenry had seen thus far. Even the women towered over him. This *master race* was Hitler's dream come true. And astonishingly, it included people of all races working as equals.

They smiled and nodded their heads in silent greeting as they passed in the corridor. Everyone seemed respectful and friendly enough. He was not prepared to meet these men and women as friends.

They reached an elevator and stepped in. *"Kontrolle,"* the doctor ordered. It took a long second for McHenry to understand that the command was meant for the elevator, then the doors closed and he quickly understood that elevators no longer needed attendants. He could feel the pull of upward and then sideways motion. Their movements felt so swift that they seemed to be moving a considerable distance. They watched an indicator move along a diagram of the vessel.

"How big is this ship?" McHenry asked.

"Over nine kilometers in length. That includes the engines. The actual living environment is less than half that. That is large enough that it might have been visible from the Earth if it was not designed to be hidden."

"Visible from where...?" But there was no time to finish the question. The doors opened and he immediately saw a black sky. The two men climbed a short stairway up into the ship's large control room. McHenry stopped momentarily and stood in awe. There didn't seem to be a ceiling. They were in a dome surrounded by stars. And right below them was the planet Earth.

*

CHAPTER 6

> "It has been claimed at times that our modern age of technology facilitates dictatorship. What we must understand is that the industries, processes, and inventions created by modern science can be used either to subjugate or liberate. The choice is up to us."
> — *Vice President Henry A. Wallace (April 9, 1944)*

McHenry stared out across the dome. This was his familiar Earth seen from a new and heretofore impossible vantage point. It couldn't be a real window, he realized, although his depth perception gave the illusion that it was. There were faint grid marks of latitude and longitude on the planet. Another more-distant blue grid marked the background of space itself. Numbers and symbols appeared in the foreground, sometimes flashing or highlighted by colorful borders. They all looked to McHenry like finely-detailed cartoon images overlapping a real sky.

The ship's large control room had at least a dozen men and women, mostly in blue Luftwaffe uniforms working at various stations. View screens surrounded every station; some displays appeared momentarily in the background of the dome and disappeared just as suddenly. The center area held two large chairs facing forward. The stern-faced *Oberführer* Mtubo was standing beside one — one of four SS officers present. The other chair was obviously meant for the *Kommandant*. This was, surprisingly to McHenry, a woman.

Luftwaffe-Oberst — Colonel, that is — Petra Volker looked very much like a woman proud of the ship she commanded. "Greetings, Lieutenant McHenry. Welcome to the *Göring*." She held out her large hand.

"Thank you," McHenry replied. He was still unsure how to address these people. He tried to consider himself a P.O.W. They shook hands firmly.

At first glance, the fair-haired and clean-cut *Kommandant* seemed to McHenry as being not being older than anyone else. She looked, perhaps, not older than thirty, judging by the smoothness of her features. But her stoic and confident manners somehow implied this was a much older woman. Only then did it start to dawn on McHenry that the Nazis had beaten mortality just as they had conquered everything else.

"I didn't realize your ship was in outer space," said McHenry.

The *Kommandant* laughed heartily. "The doctor has been babying you — eh Doctor? Do not blame him, Lieutenant. The entire crew has been, as you might say, on pins and needles. We all know this must all be quite overwhelming."

McHenry sat there feeling unexpectedly shy and hesitant. He tried to remember his P.O.W. instructions and his oath as an officer, and he searched his memory for anything he was taught that could be applied here. These people already knew his name and who-knows-what-else. No one had asked a single question. No interrogation was necessary.

He looked out over the sea to the south. "That's the Med, isn't it?"

"Yes, it's getting dark down there now."

"That's about where I ditched my plane," he said numbly. "But I guess you know that." Most of it was coming back to him now. He hoped the men got back okay.

"We knew precisely where you were going down. The ship that tried to pick you up had a log entry about you, which included the coordinates. We knew everything about you before you were selected. Traveling through time is not something we can afford to be careless about."

"I know. The doctor told me all about it."

"Then you understand the seriousness of the situation here," Mtubo interjected. "And the risks we undertook to rescue you."

"Yes, I do. I just don't understand why."

"You are a relic of history, Lieutenant," Mtubo answered with some disdain. "That makes you an interesting item."

"Do not question your good fortune," the *Kommandant* said, turning back to where Germany and western Europe were fading in the distance. "Men are giving their lives by the thousands back there. You will be remembered as a hero back home, like all the others, but you also have a second chance at life."

McHenry turned his back and looked ahead. The moon shone down on a dark planet now. "I'll have to play this one day at a time," he said finally, turning back to face the *Kommandant.*

"And what marvelous days you will have," the *Kommandant* said brightly. "Doctor!"

Dr. Evers stepped forward. "*Ja, Kommandant!*"

"Show Herr McHenry his quarters, and then let him see the ship."

"*Jawohl!*"

The *Kommandant* pivoted formally to McHenry. "The men will look in on you to ensure you learn your way about the ship. If you need any medical assistance, be sure that the doctor attends to your needs."

"Thank you, ma'am." McHenry winced slightly as he heard himself say the word *ma'am*. He needed to be respectful, and cordial, but not subservient. But he felt better about it when he saw Mtubo's stern glare. He took one last look at the land on the horizon and then followed the doctor down the short stairway to the open elevator doors.

The doctor issued a command to the elevator, and the doors closed. They moved sideways and then downward. "We have prepared a private room for you. We will stop there so that you know where it is and then we will have dinner. I am sure you are hungry."

"You've read my mind, Doctor."

"Good. *Leutnant* Vinson might be there. You will meet more of the crew over time, but it might be best if we start with the pilots."

The door to his room had his name beside it. There was a number under his name. McHenry recognized the last five digits as part of his Army serial number. The rest was not familiar.

"That is your personal number," the doctor said. "It is actually five hundred years old. The Reich integrated everyone into the system that could be accounted for — living or dead."

"I see," McHenry said numbly. He didn't like that the Reich knew who he was.

"Of course, you were long dead at the time," the doctor added.

"Listed as killed by a bird, no doubt."

The room itself was small but very comfortable. This could almost have been a stateroom on board any passenger ship. As if to highlight that point, there was even a placard with emergency instructions on the wall by the door.

The doctor showed him that the desk converts into a bed, and then remembered to explain he could adjust the temperature and lighting simply by calling out to the ship's main machine. "*Rechner, Fenster.*" The back wall dissolved into a window. Unlike the tactical view in *Kontrolle*, this looked like a clear window without the embedded graphics. They were evidently passing Asia and heading out over the Pacific.

"Wow!" McHenry exclaimed, startled. "Is that a real window?"

"No, there are no windows on this ship. The rechner is just giving us a view from one of the outside sensors. This can also show maps and pictures and even books. I am certain you will use it a lot."

McHenry remained awestruck, and was pleased that he would be able to have such a view in his room. The picture gave a perspective of depth with perfect clarity. "I'll have to remember the word *Fenster.*"

"Ah, do not worry. The rechner understands English perfectly well. Tell it what you want. It will ask for clarification if there is any chance of confusion. I think you will find some advantage to living in our time."

*

A nearly empty officers' mess was just down the hall from McHenry's quarters. He would come to find out this was the officers' mess reserved for the pilots — those who pilot the ship, and those who pilot the smaller spacecraft. The door opened automatically.

From the doorway, McHenry could see the room was clean and efficiently designed with three large portraits on the opposite wall. He recognized Adolf Hitler and Hermann Göring in two of the pictures, with likenesses appearing more muscular than the original twentieth-century men. The center portrait, slightly larger than the others, was that of a blonde woman, short-haired, and wearing a brown uniform. There could be no doubting who she was.

This *Führer* had a beautiful face, with the distracting exception of a piercing and determined stare. Had he not known better, and had she not had that stern, resolute expression, McHenry would have thought that the most powerful woman in the thirtieth-century was also in her mid-twenties.

Dr. Evers paused at the door with McHenry. "May we enter?"

"Yes, certainly," answered one of the men inside. There were only three men in the room, although it could easily accommodate two dozen. One of them was Vinson.

"Let me introduce two of our other pilots," Vinson said as McHenry and the doctor came in. "Here is Otto Barr and Lars Bamberg." Each stood as they shook McHenry's hand, and all of them towered over him even though they were bending slightly.

The three Luftwaffe pilots shared the superhuman build and height now standard in the thirtieth-century. They all seemed very much alike but for the fact that Barr was a black man, evidently a naturally jovial man, despite the fact that he sported a Hitler mustache. McHenry was still getting used to the idea of seeing the mixture of races in the Reich. He was intrigued that this society had evolved to a point where their very equality had become unremarkable. Indeed, the more obvious difference between the three was that Barr and Bamberg had Iron Crosses under their collars, and Vinson did not.

"Have you eaten yet?" asked the doctor as they took their seats around a circular table. A thankful McHenry took the chair facing away from from the portraits. It raised itself for his shorter stature automatically.

"We thought we would wait," Bamberg said. "Adolf thought you would be coming by. Are you ready for some of the best food you ever tasted?"

"What's for dinner?" asked McHenry.

"We shall see." said Vinson. He spoke a command to the rechner again. The pad in the center of the table opened and five trays appeared with piping hot food. "Pork with rice. What would you like to drink?"

"Have you got a Coke?"

"Coke?"

"Cola," Barr said. "I will have one too."

"Same," Bamberg said, and the doctor nodded, raising his thumb.

"Rechner, five colas," Vinson ordered. Five drinks appeared.

The sodas were not quite cold enough for McHenry's tastes. They were very good but they were distinctly different. The Coca-Cola Company evidently didn't survive Nazism. The food, however, was excellent. "My compliments to the chef," McHenry said.

"So what is the pilot talk nowadays?" asked the doctor.

"Our little Adolf is in love," said Barr.

"And it is the forbidden fruit," added Bamberg.

Vinson shifted uncomfortably in his seat. "It will not be improper after we return home," he mumbled, his mouth full of food.

"What is forbidden?" asked McHenry.

"Relationships with superior or subordinate officers are discouraged," answered the doctor. His lips formed a smile. "Or with anyone in the SS."

Barr's eyes widened. "Ach, you know!"

"It was obvious when the two of them brought in Herr McHenry."

Vinson turned to a confused McHenry. "She was with me on the mission to retrieve you," he said. He then looked to Barr. "And she is a very nice person. All we did was talk. It's not a relationship. She doesn't even know how I feel." The other men laughed.

"The whole ship knows how you feel," said the doctor.

36

"Mtubo?" asked Vinson meekly.

"He is not blind. Your tongue was practically on the floor."

"*Scheiss!*" exclaimed Vinson. "Do you think she knows?"

"That is not a little girl," said Bamberg.

"She has been around the town a few times," the doctor noted. "She is a hundred years older than you are."

Startled, McHenry blurted out, "You're kidding!" Again, he wondered how old everyone was.

Bamberg laughed uproariously. "That must seem strange to you. In your day, no one even lives that long."

"How long do you people live?"

"With proper care there are no limits," said the doctor.

Bamberg put his hand on McHenry's shoulder. "See, you thought you had died, and now you will live longer than anyone down there."

Those ramifications hadn't really hit McHenry until just that moment, and even then, only superficially. At twenty-four, he was a young man who had faced death, but old age would have been too far ahead of him to fully appreciate.

The camaraderie reminded him of the good times he had with his squadron, and he wondered what his friends were doing.

As a teenager, when becoming a pilot was still only a dream, McHenry had read *High Adventure*, James Norman Hall's account of his days as a World War I combat pilot. He thought about that book now, here in the officer's mess. The book concludes with Hall's crash behind enemy lines, and then his capture by the Germans. Hall spent the first evening having a friendly dinner with the German pilots. It was not a reception McHenry had ever expected for himself, and yet, here he was.

They chatted for a long time, mostly small talk. The three men were Tiger pilots. They promised he would get plenty of time to see the ships.

Adolf Vinson was the only one they called by his first name. At first, McHenry thought he might be poking fun at the name Adolf, but he soon realized it was because he was the youngest among them. At 28, Vinson was the only man close to McHenry's age. Barr made a vague hint that Vinson got this assignment through family connections, but it was never made clear, and McHenry didn't ask.

McHenry learned that Barr, of African heritage was born in Peenemünde, Germany. Bamberg was born in London. On McHenry's prompting, he found that both were in their 400s. The doctor was a mere 145.

The men laughed and the conversation quickly turned to pilot matters and Barr described his teenage years when he first learned to fly an old-style winged aircraft. "And I took it into the controlled air lanes once, mixed in the same traffic as the regular cargo transports going three times as fast as I was. The turbulence was great fun for a youth like me, but I had been in the lane less than a minute when my teacher called me, screaming his head off!"

"Very daring!" Vinson declared. "If I had tried that, my instructor would have thrown me out!"

"I was restricted for two months," Barr acknowledged. "And I was forced to march rounds every night." Then he turned more seriously to McHenry. "But at least I had a strong modern airframe. I think every pilot on this ship looks at your experience as quite challenging."

"That is correct," Vinson agreed. "We would be eager to hear some of your adventures first hand."

McHenry felt all eyes were on him. He had many stories to tell, but all he could think of was his duty, and the men he had flown with. "I'm afraid I can't discuss our flight operations," he said blankly. "That would be classified." It all came out almost automatically, and he knew it sounded strange to these men, but he felt it was the right thing to do.

The men were taken aback. There were a few long seconds of silence until Barr guffawed, but that was quickly followed by an approving grin from Bamberg. Vinson and the doctor remained silent for a few seconds more.

"You are a good man," said Bamberg.

The doctor was the next to speak. "Gentlemen, Herr McHenry had seen what might have been jets or rocket planes."

"No," Vinson said, apparently happy to change the subject. "That is too soon. They were not flying in your area."

"There are still only test flights," said Barr.

"I don't know what they are," McHenry said. "Nobody does. All I know is that we've seen some very fast aircraft."

"Never heard of anything you would not recognize as an airplane," said Bamberg. "Are they combat aircraft? Have they ever attacked anyone?"

"Not to my knowledge."

"What do they look like?" asked Vinson.

"Round and silver and very fast."

"*Traumsehen?*" asked the doctor.

"Yes," Bamberg concurred.

The men left their plates and they all walked to the doctor's dispensary. McHenry didn't like the idea of a medical experiment, but Vinson promised he would find it interesting. He took a seat on the edge of the first bed.

"This is a very old technology," said Vinson.

The doctor spoke a command, and a cabinet opened to reveal a metal elliptical ring. The doctor fitted it to McHenry's head. "Do not worry, it will not harm you."

A view screen over the bed lit up with a bright moving pattern of shapes. The men gathered around and watched it form patterns.

"You must concentrate on the craft that you saw," the doctor said. "Try to imagine it in your mind and then watch the pictures. The machine is measuring the part of your brain that recognizes images. It will redraw these designs until it senses that you see something familiar in them."

The pattern turned and shifted several times, and changed into circles, ellipses, triangles, and innumerable polygons and then returned to ellipses again. They stretched and flattened until it came closer to approximating the oval form of the ship he had seen. It gradually developed a three-dimensional texture. The colors stopped changing, and then the image finally resolved itself into a picture as vivid as McHenry's memory.

"Ach!" Bamberg stammered.

"That's it!" McHenry exclaimed. He was so surprised to see that the machine could create the picture that he didn't register the shock on the other faces. Barr and Bamberg ran out the door.

Vinson slapped his hand to the swastika on this collar. "*Kontrolle!*" he shouted.

"*Ja, Vinson,*" a voice replied.

Vinson spoke quickly in German.

"What's going on?" McHenry asked the doctor. "What was that thing?"

"The enemy," the doctor whispered. "Our enemy."

*

CHAPTER 7

"Once before in our lifetime, we fell into disunity and
became ineffective in world affairs by reason of it.
Should this happen again, it will be a tragedy to you
and to your children and the world for generations."
— *Secretary of State Cordell Hull, (April 9, 1944)*

Vinson ushered McHenry back to *Kontrolle*. He refused to utter a
word about this enemy of theirs. "I'll explain later," he had promised,
despite McHenry's attempts to make him share a hint. The corridors
were empty, the entire crew at their alert stations.

Kommandant Volker and *Oberführer* Mtubo were obviously prepared
for them. The starboard side of the dome had a sky blue background
with a full size image of McHenry's sighting. The silver spaceship
seemed to hang there outside the dome, motionless, in three-
dimensions.

A second SS man stood beside Mtubo. A white man with dark
hair. McHenry had not seen him before. The black uniform had
nearly similar oak leaf markings, a rank just one level below Mtubo's.

"Herr McHenry, this is *Standartenführer* Stern," said the
Kommandant. "He is the project's research director."

Stern wasted no time. He gestured to the image on the dome. "Is
this what you saw, with no prompting from anyone?"

McHenry instinctively identified Stern as a no-nonsense worm of
a man. His eyes could look straight through McHenry, as though
studying him like a bug. "That's exactly how I remember it," he
replied.

"We added no details whatsoever, *Herr Standartenführer*," offered
Vinson. "We have not even discussed the Grauen yet. We were
ordered to keep things light for the first few days."

Mtubo muttered something in German that McHenry didn't
understand.

"Rechner, display for us a *Grauschiff null neun,*" ordered Stern. A new picture appeared in the air. It was an image similar to the one the machine had drawn, with exhaust vents beneath it. "Could this be what you saw?"

"I only saw it for a second," McHenry admitted. "But I don't remember those holes along the bottom."

Mtubo issued a command in German and the picture changed again. "And this?"

"Exactly like that."

"A Geier," Mtubo said. "Definitely the older model."

"So, they did not follow us here," the *Kommandant* acknowledged. "Assuming we are correct about ship classes."

"No matter," Stern concluded. "It is virtually certain that this one did not alter history as we know it."

"Why so?" the *Kommandant* asked.

"It is the certainty of cause and effect," said Stern. "An event like Herr McHenry's sighting of the Grauen would have affected the timing of his subsequent actions. Even if the timing difference was small, it still would have affected fractions of seconds spent shaving, eating breakfast, and countless other deviations in how he lived and worked in the twentieth-century. For most people, on most days, this might not make much of a difference. The small affect on the action of an ordinary soldier would be corrected once he concentrates on combat. But Herr McHenry is an aviator, flying a craft by hand. The cumulative effect would certainly have been enough to affect his flight path into the bird that disabled him."

McHenry had listened intently and understood at least part of it. "You mean, if I didn't see that ship last January, I wouldn't have been thinking of it yesterday, and so I might have taken an extra second or two, more or less, to get to altitude, and that would have been enough to miss the bird."

"Correct, *Leutnant.*"

"But what's the point?" McHenry asked. "Wouldn't I have been better off if I hadn't seen that ship?"

"Probably so," Stern replied. "But the real issue is for us to know that our history has not been changed. Everything is progressing as it should be."

"Not quite," Mtubo interrupted. "The sighting was not in our records. Why was this not reported?"

"It was," McHenry stated. "I was also debriefed by two British officers."

Stern had a faraway look. "We will have to look into that. This one discrepancy could be a boon to our research here."

"Thank you Herr McHenry," the *Kommandant* said. "But we are still faced with the reality of the presence of Grauen in this time period. Should we alter the mission profile to *Platt Zwei, Oberführer?*"

"*Ja,*" Mtubo concurred.

The *Kommandant* turned to address Vinson. "Thank you gentlemen, you are dismissed."

"*Jawohl!*" said Vinson.

The *Kommandant* turned to shout orders to the crew in *Kontrolle*." The image of the Grauen ship disappeared, and they were surrounded by stars again, with the Earth below. She turned briefly to McHenry and Vinson, smiled and nodded, dismissing them.

Mtubo stopped the two men at the stairs. "Good work," he said. "You have been a tremendous help, Herr McHenry. We will summon you if we have more questions. *Heil Renard!*"

"*Heil Renard!*" returned Vinson.

McHenry wondered how soon he would be expected to say that, should he not manage to escape. The thought disturbed him. He looked down at the blue uniform he was wearing and questioned whether he should have kept his mouth shut about the ship. The words echoed through his mind, *You have been a tremendous help.*

Vinson led the way through the doors to the elevator. "What's going on?" McHenry asked. He had wanted to learn something about the Grauen.

"We will go to the hangar deck," Vinson said as the elevator doors closed behind them. "*Flugzeughalle,*" he ordered. "I think you would like to see the Tigers, which is the class of work ships we use. They are very likely going to send one out now. We have satellites, or buoys if you will, in orbit around the Earth. They look down and record history for our analysts. They are nearly invisible, but some more so than others. We cannot allow the Grauen to find and capture the most detectable ones. Our procedures mandate that those be retrieved now. The *Kommandant* will likely be taking us to a higher orbit so that we can continue monitoring events in Europe directly."

"Why move higher?"

The elevator doors opened. Vinson continued as they walked down the long hallway. "At that altitude, we orbit the Earth at the same rate that it turns. Then the ship can remain stationary directly over the same spot, focused on the European continent, without expending energy."

He took lengthy strides that made it awkward for McHenry to keep up. Vinson continued, "There is one disadvantage. It is a predictable orbit. We assume the enemy will scan there first. That is why this goes against Luftwaffe doctrine. But with a smaller pattern of satellites, the SS will want a constant view over Europe."

They reached an intersection with an open hatch in the corner. It went to a tube that ran vertically up to the hangar. Vinson jumped in and grabbed the ladder. Suddenly weightless, he held on effortlessly with one hand. "Has the doctor taken you here before?"

"No," McHenry answered, waiting in the doorway. He knew something was strange in the tube. Vinson was barely holding onto the ladder.

"Just follow me. There is no gravity in here. It is quite normal, so do not be afraid." Then he climbed up out of sight.

Not knowing what to expect, McHenry jumped and tried to grab the ladder as casually as Vinson had done. He missed the intended rung and clumsily grabbed onto the next one. His coordination was unprepared for the drop in gravitation. He held tight. The experience felt like the whole ship was falling. Mindful that Vinson was watching, McHenry maintained his composure.

"Are you all right down there?"

McHenry looked up at Vinson floating in the tube several yards above him. "Just fine. It's only a bit of a surprise, that's all." It really was worse than that but it felt better after he closed his eyes momentarily and could imagine he was really falling. The weightlessness in the tube confused his senses.

"Dr. Evers had warned that you might not like it in here," said Vinson. "We can go back and see the Tigers after you have fully acclimated yourself. I understand it must be hard if you have never been weightless before."

"No, I can handle it." McHenry climbed one rung at a time, hugging the ladder with his legs. Actually, he had been weightless before. He just didn't want to tell Vinson it was while dive-bombing. It's different without an aircraft fuselage around him. He looked back down at the tube's entrance. "I don't understand the physics of the sudden drop off. That's not supposed to be possible."

"You have time to learn," said Vinson, almost at the hatch.

They didn't have far to go. The hatch above wasn't more than twenty yards away, and they moved swiftly. It opened when Vinson was nearby, and McHenry hurried his pace. They floated through to the hangar deck. The entire section had no gravity.

"Now I know why nobody wears hats," said McHenry.

The enormous hangar deck was a busy place. Men and women, all wearing Luftwaffe blue, worked on terminal stations or at one of the spacecraft parked at one of the three mooring latches. Each black ship was 100 feet long with no visible windows. A dark gray swastika, Luftwaffe emblem and serial number adorned the tail sections. One of the latches was vacant. McHenry guessed a ship was out on a mission.

Each of the spacecraft moors rested flat against the curvature of the entire ship. There was no real sense of up and down. The entire area was weightless, and people worked at stations facing in all directions. Vinson and McHenry clung to one of the railings that stretched across the hangar, but McHenry noted that some of the linemen wore control belts and could fly about the hangar.

"That looks like fun."

"Oh, it is. Every child gets to play like that. Even when you grow up, you never get bored of it. But it is dangerous to play in here when there is flight activity. There is a Tiger out retrieving satellites already.

This other is being serviced, but they should not be long." Vinson pointed to men working near the door. "When they are done, we will have a look inside." They settled in to a spot along the railing where they could wait.

"Now," McHenry began, "what about the Grauen?"

"Ah, the Grauen," Vinson sighed. "We think the Grauen have been watching us since soon after Earth's first radio transmissions. No one is really sure. They are considerably more advanced than we are and have probably been traveling the stars for millions of years."

"Millions of years!" McHenry repeated, looking again at the ships on the dock. "I can't imagine what kind of society that must be."

"And that is the problem. Neither can we. They don't talk to us, and we can't find their home planet. A barrier was recently discovered in space that no one has ever returned from. We think they come from that direction."

"A barrier? Like, a wall in space?"

"Yes," Vinson said, nodding. "We call it the Far Wall. It was discovered five years ago, and it is vast. Every ship that went into it just disappeared. We even sent survey ships to the edge, but they disappeared, too."

"Is that even possible?" asked McHenry, more a statement than a question.

"No, it is not possible in any way we understand. And we understand a lot."

"Who started the war?" McHenry asked after a pause. He liked Vinson but assumed the Reich was at fault.

Yet Vinson was not playing along. "This is not much of a war. There had been many incidents over time, beginning with the first stories about sightings of their ships and abductions. It did not become a major concern until they destroyed a Luftwaffe ship on the ground in Djibouti. That was five hundred years ago, and we have been shooting at them ever since."

"Djibouti, Africa?"

"Yes. It was the best place to launch rockets back in the late twentieth-century. Any failures fall safely into the Indian Ocean. And it took less fuel to reach orbit from central Africa because it is so much nearer the equator than Peenemünde. You see, they needed every advantage back in the early times. It is not important at all now but most of the large Luftwaffe spacecraft are still assembled there."

The linemen had turned toward the adjacent spacecraft and jetted off in that direction.

"Let's go," said Vinson. He sprang forward and floated along the handrail. McHenry followed, feeling that he was finally getting the hang of it.

The hatch was a circular opening with no sign of an actual door. A ladder extended from inside, with some German lettering along the side in gray print. McHenry could not read what it said, but it reminded him of the "NO STEP" warnings stenciled on his own aircraft. He almost felt he was in familiar territory.

They crawled through the open hatch and followed a narrow crawlspace to the cockpit, which was dimly bathed in a red light. Two seats faced forward, although it was large enough to accommodate four. They stared at a grid-squared wall in what appeared to be a distance larger than McHenry knew the Tiger could be. Once fully inside, McHenry turned behind and saw that the grid extended fully 360 degrees behind him as well. He reached back to feel the wall that he could not see. It was all an optical illusion of a sort. Even the way he came from was now part of the grid.

"It's like magic," McHenry said.

"Yes," Vinson said, smiling. "It is a little like magic to me, too, and I know how it works."

Each seat had two control sticks. Any other controls and gauges would be on a small panel before them, except for a panel on the side that retracted when Vinson pushed it. "The SS officer uses that for scanning and library functions."

McHenry nodded but kept looking at the indicators on the main panel before them, trying to guess what it could all mean.

Vinson swung into one seat. A black strip came out from underneath and held onto his chest and waist. McHenry hesitated only a second and then took the other seat. The strip was soft, holding him firmly but comfortably in place.

"*Rechner, aufleuchten!*" Vinson commanded. The grid disappeared, replaced by a view from inside the hangar.

McHenry looked behind him. It was as though the rest of the Tiger had disappeared around them. But like the view in *Kontrolle*, there were reticles and grid marks and numbers around the view."

"Where did it all go? Are we invisible?"

"It's still there," Vinson explained. "This is a composite from the sensors. Or, I guess you might think of them as cameras."

"I don't know what you mean by 'composite.'"

"There is a sensor array all around this ship, with many different views. The rechner assembles this image from all those pictures to make it appear it is one view all around the ship."

McHenry focused on the reticles and grid marks overlaying the view. "So this is really something like a picture that the machine draws for us?"

"Very much like that, but it is all based upon what is really out there."

"I see," said McHenry, now willing to accept the view as it was. It didn't matter that he still wasn't sure whether it was real or fake. It was useful. He put his hand on the stick. "So how do I fly this thing?"

"It is only a little bit like an airplane. We do not rely only on the stick control." Vinson reached to the panel. "These are the vital engine functions. If we were about to leave on a mission, the rechner would show this as the engines were initializing, and then again whenever I needed to know more details than were displayed on the dome background."

McHenry stared at the panel, attempting to make sense of it. He began to see that the numbers, some of them changing as he watched, were like the needles on his gauges. The legends were mostly abbreviations, all of it in German.

"How do you start the engine?" asked McHenry.

"It is not one engine. A Tiger has over twenty-four thousand drivers, or what you might call engines."

"Is there no thrust from this engine?"

"Exactly. It is a reactionless drive."

McHenry's eyes narrowed. That was an impossibility, he thought, but he had seen too many of them already. "Okay, how do these engines start up?"

"They start in phases. We could bring out this display and start each phase ourselves, but the rechner does that better than a man ever could. The rechner usually knows the mission we are assigned. It will start the engines when we give the command and set up the navigation. It could take us all the way there and back if we want it to. The stick is for making quick flight adjustments, and for manual combat maneuvers."

"It seems to me that the machine does a lot of the work for you," McHenry surmised. "I guess there is a lot for it to do."

"Well, it is not like it was in your day. A pilot has a different role than just flying the craft. You probably need to become more acquainted with the rechners."

"I guess so," said McHenry, realizing that was going to be his next task.

A sense of inadequacy overwhelmed him. He had thought this could have been his best chance to escape. He was alone with only one other man on a spacecraft that could very likely be capable of taking him down to his base in Italy. Perhaps even straight to the United States. Or maybe directly to Berlin, he thought, where he could drop a powerful space weapon on Hitler's Nazi bunker... If only he could fly this thing now.

Besides, he realized, Vinson was too kind a soul to bash his brains in, even if he hadn't been so much larger — and almost certainly much stronger.

"Have you ever flown one of these in combat?" he asked.

"Never," replied Vinson. "Grauen sightings are rare. The Reich has had no other enemies for over five hundred years. There might be one reported every three or four months, but I haven't been so lucky."

"Really? Don't Barr and Bamberg have Iron Crosses? How did they get those?"

"My friend, you have no experience of our times," said Vinson. "They have been flying for a couple hundred years. That is long enough to have seen combat. Perhaps not as much as you have, but they have seen more than enough."

McHenry allowed that to stand. It was clearly true. The Tiger may have had a stick and something like a window, but it was not an airplane. He had a thousand years to catch up on.

"See this," said Vinson, fiddling with the panel. The background image disappeared completely, replaced by a field of stars with the Earth below.

McHenry held back expressing his astonishment, but he did look behind to see if the *Göring* was anywhere nearby.

"We are now in game or simulator mode," Vinson explained. "We use this for training. I will be able to show you how we do things."

"You mean, we hadn't really moved, and we're still in the hangar," said McHenry, unsteadily. The only comparison he could think of was Hollywood.

They practiced flying through space while Vinson explained the simple basics. They spent ten minutes working this way, and McHenry slowly got a feel for the controls.

"When you first learned to fly, did you make passes over the airfield?"

"Yes, they're called touch-and-goes."

Vinson reconfigured the simulator again. This time McHenry could understand what Vinson was doing even if he couldn't quite follow along. They were now positioned at low orbit just at the edge of space, at a steep descent.

"We will do a touch-and-go over Berlin," Vinson said. "You couldn't practice like this in real life, but in simulation, we can."

McHenry's breath caught. He understood that Vinson was being friendly, but his own sense of duty picked up again. He needed to learn this so that, perhaps one day soon, he might take a Tiger for real. *It wouldn't be a touch-and-go,* he hoped. *It would be a bombing run.*

"And as you can see," Vinson continued, "we can start the flight anywhere. It could take hours to get to this point in the landing sequence were this a real flight. Now, watch the angle."

They progressed steeply. McHenry would later learn the different types of approaches, but this one was standard. Vinson would explain the procedure while McHenry imagined, if he escapes, doing this for real. But the dream fell apart when Berlin came into view. It was not the Berlin of 1944. The Tiger was simulating the Berlin of 2968.

Even from the distance, there was no doubting its majesty. Continuing the approach, its myriad skyscrapers became visible.

"It's beautiful," McHenry gasped.

Only then did Vinson recognize the nature of McHenry's amazement. "Oh, I should have started with the flyover. I guess you were expecting the twentieth-century version. The Tiger knows the current year but its programming is not aware of the full situation, as it would be if on a real mission. For security reasons, their memories are cleared after each mission."

They broke off the approach and did the flyover. Later, they reset and did Paris and New York City before simulating a return home to the *Göring*.

Göring had not become visible until it blossomed into view less than two kilometers away, at which point it filled the sky. Even then its appearance had to be enhanced by the machine. This was the first time McHenry had seen the outside hull of *Göring* — a long cigar-shape surrounded in black netting.

"That net is the reason we could not see it right away," Vinson explained. "The material format is called *unterkarbon*. It distorts any light that passes through it."

"So that ship is invisible?" asked McHenry.

"From a sufficient distance, yes. We think even the Grauen cannot see it. The Tigers have them too. They extend outward, and then retract as they're brought into the ship."

McHenry circled the ship for a second look. The black net was woven in a geometric pattern formed out of triangles. He instinctively knew that the geometry must be essential, but couldn't imagine how it may work.

The docking maneuver was easy. They simply ordered the rechner to take it in. There was no discernible point where the netting was being retracted. McHenry wondered whether the simulation skips that step, or if the machine just handles it as smoothly as it does so much else.

It had been a long day, and Vinson had promised the doctor that McHenry would get to bed early. He led the way out of the hangar, back into the main part of the ship. McHenry had become accustomed to zero-gravity, but was happy to be standing on a firm deck once again.

Once there, the door to his room slid open. McHenry paused at the entrance. "How does it know I'm going in there?"

"The rechner makes judgments based upon which way you are going," Vinson answered. "It probably also watches what direction you are looking at. And, of course, it knows that is your door."

McHenry was not comfortable with a machine that could know so much. "How does it know which direction I'm looking at?"

Vinson laughed. "The rechner can see and hear everything in the ship."

McHenry pretended to laugh along with him, but he wasn't sure if that was meant as a straight answer.

"If you need to know anything, just call for the rechner."

"Thanks."

The doors closed behind McHenry and he was alone for the first time that day. Or as alone as he could be with a machine that could see and hear everything he does.

"Rechner," he said. Then he stood there while trying to remember the word for the window command.

After a few seconds, a voice came out of the air. "Waiting."

"Is that you, machine?"

"Yes. Waiting." The rechner spoke with a slightly unhuman form of a proper-sounding British accent.

"I want to see the window again."

The window appeared in the wall. They were much higher now and the curvature of the Earth was more pronounced. The ship seemed to be moving too slowly to discern any motion.

"What was the word for that?"

"Window."

"No. I mean, what was the German word for that?"

"*Fenster.*"

He sat down, stared out the window, and wondered what he would do next.

"Rechner, what is going on down there right now?"

"Germany is currently at war against an alliance of hostile nations. It is night in Europe. Action has generally been postponed until morning in all the major points of conflict."

"Can you see in the dark?"

The ground seemed to become illuminated. It was suddenly like daytime.

"Wow!" McHenry exclaimed. He could suddenly imagine new possibilities. "Can you magnify the picture on the screen?"

"That function is restricted."

"Why?"

"Detailed live event data is classified."

Frustrated, he felt like he had been thrust back to the reality of his situation. He was a prisoner of war after all. After a few moments of thought, he tried reasoning with the machine. "Why can you tell me what is going on down there but not show me?"

"Analysis of current events is retrieved from unclassified historical data."

He pondered that for a moment. "What you're saying is, the only way you can tell me what's going on is by looking at your history books?"

"That is a correct analogy."

McHenry was intrigued. Their secrecy confirmed for him that, with a telescopic view, the Nazis can tell so much more than they want him to know. He leaned back in his chair, only momentarily stymied. "Rechner," he said, hoping to take a new tack. "Can you tell me what will happen in the morning?"

"American and British bombing campaigns will resume in Europe. Odessa will fall to the Soviet Army. President Roosevelt begins a rest period. Would you like detailed information?"

"No, rechner. Thanks." The possibility of finding out the future repulsed him. This wasn't a parlor game or a carnival fortuneteller. It was the realization that the world he knew, loved, hated, suffered, and defended will come to a bitter defeat. He sat for a long time contemplating what had become of him, his country, his family and his friends. Most of all, he thought about how he might escape from this place. And he wondered what Parker would do if he were here.

Then he did something he had not done since he was a child. He prayed a silent prayer.

*

Oberführer Klaus Mtubo stood by the full-wall view panel in his large private office looking down over the Earth below. In moments of quiet reflection, some men might prefer to relax beside a pastoral scene from home. Not Mtubo. His view of the Earth was overlaid with a Luftwaffe chart linked in with event data from the main watch room. He was a man of duty. He served the *Führer*. Her defense, and the defense of the Reich, always came first, even on occasions when he chose to take a respite.

Helmut Stern's chime sounded at the door.

"Enter," Mtubo commanded.

Stern stepped in, looking uncharacteristically disturbed. "*Heil Renard!*" he said quickly. Mtubo acknowledged and returned the greeting, and Stern waited until the door closed before relaxing his posture. Although the two men were longtime friends, Stern always preserved the dignity of his friend's superior rank when in the presence of others.

"You will not believe this, Klaus," he said. "I have the finding."

Mtubo turned to the side and glanced at the project overview now on the panel. Everything appeared in order. "Is this about the Americaner's Grauen sighting?"

"Yes," said Stern. "This won't show on the main status boards until it is checked against the plot. The reports are still preliminary."

"Does it show the Grauen?" asked Mtubo.

"Yes, it does. It was indeed a Geier. We have tracked its entire flight path. The satellite that recorded it would not have been analyzed until May. We put in a rush order."

"Good," said Mtubo. "What was the problem?"

"The Geier was in the atmosphere thirty-two minutes. It did not actively interfere with events. Then it went back into orbit before starting its interstellar drive. There was no attempt to hide. I am certain we would have seen it during a normal review."

"And?" Mtubo prodded, knowing his friend often takes too long to make a point.

"Just one more item before I get to the issue," Stern promised. "There were a number of eyewitnesses. Most were of the sort whose occupations and subsequent lives would not be affected. We believe their influence on events was negligible." A time chart was added to the panel.

Mtubo looked at the chart while Stern went on.

"Do you know what happened to the English intelligence officers that the Americaner said he spoke to? They were killed at sea. The records of his entry to the base were lost. The records of their request to see him were also logged, and those logs were stored. But our extrapolation posits them as discarded at the end of the war."

Mtubo started laughing a deep belly laugh. "Not surprising. You know that the old English were always very naive about information. They threw away everything that they in their worldview thought of as unimportant. They were like the Americaners this way. If it was not about money, it was not important to them."

They both shared a laugh.

"But you had something else?" asked Mtubo.

"Yes. We have collected more historical data than we had dreamed. I would like to ask that we retain some of the larger satellites that we just scheduled for shutdown."

"We put these rules in place for a reason, Helmut. Some of them were at your urging."

"If the mission needs to go a second time, it will need to evade this first mission. The *Kommandant* says this is risky, and I believe her."

"If we continue this level of progress, there will be no need for a second pass."

"Do the best you can without the large satellites. There is too much at risk."

Stern nodded. "We will make it work. Do not forget my initial conclusion that history is unchanged. The fact remains that the Americaner's day would not have ended the same way if he had never seen that Grauen."

Mtubo turned to face the portrait of Adolf Hitler hanging in its customary position beside that of Katrina Renard, the current *Führer*. The proud image gave him some comfort now as he considered the mysterious clockwork of nature that led great men and women to their destiny.

*

CHAPTER 8

"The liberty of the whole Earth depends on the outcome of this contest."
— *The Negro Soldier, (film released April 10, 1944)*

Monday, April 10, 1944

McHenry awoke slumped in the chair, still wearing the clothes he had been given the day before. The shirt and trousers had relaxed their fit while he slept, making for a comfortable sleep. The Earth was still below, outside the machine-generated window displayed before him. The false illumination of the planet was now gone. Europe was back in its cloudy daylight; and to the east he could see the Italian peninsula. The skies were clear. The fighting must have resumed. He was off to a late start.

After a quick fifty pushups, he jumped into the small bathroom for a shower. He squinted at the mirror image projected on the wall. It was the first time he had looked at himself since his arrival. The curious realization that he didn't need to shave and — judging by the smooth appearance of his face — may never need to again, startled him until he noticed his teeth. They had the gleaming white shine that everyone else had. He looked closer. No more fillings. No imperfections. *When did they get a chance to do that?* He couldn't help but smile. He was already immortal, he guessed.

His clothes were gone from the chair and a fresh suit lay on the open dispenser drawer. It was another reminder of the endlessly convenient future he would live in. He dressed again, and the blue suit tightened after it was on him. The joy of his immortality was suddenly gone. He was an American soldier, he admonished himself. He must find a way to resist.

He stood and stretched, facing the wall with the emergency directions placard and a hopeful smile formed upon his lips. The placard was written in German but the diagrams of passageways were easy to follow. Arrows traced the way down the hall and up a ladder to what was obviously a spaceship's equivalent of a lifeboat. It was a way out. Then as if to sanctify an escape attempt, the door opened the instant McHenry looked at it.

The corridor was empty. He walked down the hall until he reached a corner, and entered the tube. His adjustment to zero-gravity was quick this time. This was the same tube that led to the Tigers, but he went downward about 200 feet to the end of the tube, pausing at each floor to be sure no one would see him pass by.

A thick hatch opened automatically at the end. The center of the seven lifeboat hatches was directly before him. That one opened automatically and rapidly closed again once he was inside.

The lifeboat interior was more spherical, but tapered at the opposite end. Almost every available square foot contained a cushioned seat with a feed for a seat belt and shoulder harness. But McHenry didn't take time for a close examination of the seating arrangements. He followed the handholds to the controls at the front of the cabin. There were two rows of blank buttons at each pilot's seat, but only one control stick. Yesterday's piloting lesson would be useful here. It wasn't like the Tiger's wraparound cockpit dome, but the main panel looked familiar enough. The blank view screen reminded him of the wall in his quarters.

"Rechner, *Fenster*." It displayed a view similar to the one he had from his room but from a different section of the sky.

He ignored the seat belt. There wasn't time, and Vinson had said there would be no sense of motion from the reactionless drive. If this worked at all, he could strap himself in later. He set one hand on the stick and scanned the panel for anything familiar. He spotted the engine controls, albeit only one bank of engines. *Close enough*, he thought.

Without a second thought, he pressed the control on the panel, hoping for something, any movement at all. But an "X" appeared with an unfamiliar German word beside it. He scanned the panel further. Then he remembered chocks, the wooden blocks used to keep a parked aircraft from rolling out of place. He must be locked by the *Göring*. Frustratingly, it only made sense. They wouldn't have allowed him to go off on his own if they didn't think it safe.

Undaunted, he tried again. And again, scrolling through options on the panel, some in German words and symbols he recognized from yesterday, and some he couldn't even guess at. Nothing changed the power levels.

They can't have thought of everything.

McHenry would not stop thinking. Both hands on the panel, he went through every option available. Engine functions, instruments, something he thought might be beacons, which he imagined could be useful, and then he spotted the radios. There were many options he had never heard of — frequencies off the scale, and a variety of modulation methods — but he saw one band he had used every day. That, he realized, was his next best option. He looked at the screen ahead to verify he had a direct line of sight for a transmission to Cercola, Italy. *Someone at the 99th would recognize my voice.*

"The radios won't work here," said a feminine voice behind him.

He turned around to face a woman floating at the entranceway. She had fair skin and short raven-black hair. Yet, she had a black SS uniform similar to what the men wore. And she smiled, looking at him like the mother of a little boy who had been caught with his hand in a cookie jar.

"And you'll need someone ranking higher than me to authorize a launch." She had been speaking in a distinctly American dialect. She tugged on the railing and pushed herself forward.

McHenry frowned. "If you're here to arrest me, you're too late. I'm not going anywhere yet."

"No," she laughed. "Our security is absolutely solid. We wouldn't let you run loose through the ship if escape wasn't impossible." She grabbed the seat beside him and gracefully pulled her long legs into a sitting position. "But to tell you the truth, we would have been a little disappointed if you didn't try to escape. I, myself, would have been very disappointed."

She was studying him in an imperious manner. "You might have gotten away if this ship was on a regular mission. I don't know if the Luftwaffe ordinarily locks the escape pods. But this mission is different. We'd all prefer to die here in orbit rather than risk contaminating history."

"It wouldn't bother me a bit either," McHenry remarked.

"That's not very nice," she laughed, apparently brushing off his anger. She reached over to shake his hand. "My name is Kathy Dale. I was on the flight to recover you."

Startled, McHenry understood who this was. *This must be the woman Vinson was smitten with.* Now he understood why. She may be over one hundred years old, but she had the perpetual youth and vitality shared by everyone he had seen. She was truly beautiful, and exhibited a confident attitude. But, beautiful as she was, there was that hideous pitch-black Nazi uniform... He took her hand cautiously, and shook it firmly.

"*Oberführer* Mtubo asked me to look in on you today," she continued. "He thought you might appreciate meeting someone from North America. I was born and raised in Chicago."

"Then what's a nice lady like you doing in a uniform like that?" Nothing he had seen, not even a black Nazi, had prepared him for speaking with an American in that uniform. And a lady at that.

"Oh, I know all this must be very disorienting. One day Germany is your enemy, and then you wake up and everything's different."

"It's not different at all." McHenry gestured toward the planet below them on the view screen. "The war is still going on, isn't it?"

"I'm sorry, Sam," Dale said. "This is old history for us. And it's over for you, too. It ended for you the moment your plane sank into the sea. You must accept this. Be glad you're still alive! You've lived to see that America will recover from its defeat, and the American racism you and your ancestors have suffered through will be defeated as well."

"I'm a soldier," he reminded her. "I swore an oath."

But it was even more than that. Much more. Black troops were often relegated to non-combat positions in this war. The men in his own squadron had to prove themselves time and time again. The *right to fight* was something that he, his friends, and those before them had all worked hard for. He couldn't let them down. Then there were the squadron commander, and even a few of the white officers who had supported their training. He couldn't let any of them down. He just wouldn't.

"You fought to the best of your ability," Dale responded. "History remembers you that way. And even if you returned, what could you do to change the outcome? Germany will still win the war, and the United States will still accept peace. The Great Depression will resume. Did you ever realize how deeply mired in debt your President Roosevelt has put the country to fight his immoral war? Believe me, you don't need to go back to that. You'd be just another unemployed black man in an America where hypocrisy and unfairness are commonplace."

"Don't tell me Nazis outlawed unfairness," he scoffed.

"Who else could?"

"You mean, it takes a dictator."

"No, it takes a reordering of society. Just as war is a cause that can discipline a society, military values can advance society in peaceful ways. We take the direction of a society out of the hands of the oligarchs of wealth, and channel it into more productive purposes for the whole nation."

She paused, but only for a moment before continuing. "I will concede that the National Socialist Party of this time, that which is down there now," she gestured toward the image of the Earth outside, "regards its own form of nationalism as confined to the German-speaking race. But they have always been reaching out to new allies, not just the Italians and other Europeans, but South America, the Arabs, and of course, Japan. The Reich broadcasts radio news around the world in twelve languages. Surely, you must know that, right now, there are SS troops forming from countries all over Europe, not just Germany. And that's just a start, today, in the national socialism of 1944."

"Wait a second," said McHenry, pondering her idealistic lecture. "How can a world state call itself nationalist?"

"It was an evolution. You call yourself an American but the first several generations of Americans thought of themselves first as citizens of their separate states. They formed the nation only when they thought it necessary to close ranks. Today, in this twentieth-century, bonds are already forming among the foreign SS corps. Most of the Waffen-SS is currently non-German even here, now, in 1944.

They have many French and Scandinavian SS troops, as well as Bosnian Muslims. After the war, they will serve their own nations, following the customs learned from the SS."

"And black Nazis?" he demanded.

"Sam," she sighed. "If you're going to try to get along here, you should at least get one thing straight: We don't call ourselves 'Nazis.' The critics did. Some followers in other nations did, but the main party never did. We are *national socialists*."

"Very well then, I'm sorry," he said, barely concealing a smirk. "Then what about black *national socialists*? How long have they been around?"

She smiled again. "There is one in America right now, after a fashion."

He raised an eyebrow.

"Have you heard of Lawrence Dennis?"

The name sounded vaguely familiar — then he remembered reading it in the papers. "You mean the isolationist? That anti-war nut-case? He's not white?"

"He's a *nationalist*," she corrected. "He's not a member of the Party, of course, being an American, but he is associated with the cause. He's been to Germany before the war and visited high party officials.

He stared.

"And yes," she said. "In case you're wondering, his mother was black."

"It doesn't count if he's been passing for white," McHenry shrugged.

"That's only today. There will be more. A lot can happen in a thousand years, Sam." She allowed that to sink in.

He knew that much was true. A lot *can* happen in a thousand years. But this was still 1944. He couldn't stop glancing down at the swastika on her arm. It was a long time before McHenry spoke. "Okay, then. What are SS officers doing here on this ship? I thought you people were state security and secret police."

"The SS started that way, back in the 1920s, when it was a small unit that guarded the Party leaders. The name, '*Schutzstaffel*,' means 'defense corps.' But they quickly expanded after Adolf Hitler came to power, and then expanded further still when the war started. But we've always been, primarily, the hand of the *Führer*. As such, the SS works in many scientific fields. That's why we're here. This is a scientific expedition."

"I believe everything up to where you said this is about science."

"Nothing new about that, Sam. Even in your time, the SS has doctors expanding the frontiers of medical research."

"Yeah, I'll bet."

"We are all beneficiaries of that science — including you, in your resuscitation."

"Apparently so," he slowly acknowledged, but really wanting only to change the subject. "Well then, how soon does Germany take over the United States?"

"It's not Germany by itself. It's the Reich that grows and attracts people of like minds. It becomes much more than just Germany during the next century. The United States doesn't join for over a hundred years, and then, initially, as a pact member. When it happens, it will do so willingly.

"As you said, we started as, and in some sense still are, a nationalist movement. You know that Italy was an ally; Japan still is; and Spain is a friend. These are nationalist countries, each distinct peoples with similar national ideologies. After the war, more will become like that. Nationalist movements will bloom all over the world, holding down the capitalists and kicking out the Bolsheviks. People in South America and the Middle East are preparing to do that now.

"The United States will follow behind them, but not right away. Your economic depression will resume first. The country wasted so much money on this immoral war. Unfortunately, America will lose its will to succeed, and with that, the technological edge it had in recent decades. It will become weak economically and militarily. That can only last for so long before the people react, just as they did in Germany. Eventually, Americans will look to the Reich for hope and inspiration, and they will find it. Once the entire world is working the same way, it is only natural that we start working together."

McHenry didn't buy her story. It was apparent to him that the country was out of the Depression. He didn't think it was going to reverse the process but he wasn't going to argue any of it yet.

"And the war?" he asked.

Her voice became tender. "For Japan, which Americans should have considered the real war, that war goes on for another year. The war in Europe ends this year. Roosevelt will die of a stroke."

McHenry shook his head, first shocked at the loss of the President, and then startled by his own reaction. He loved President Roosevelt. His whole squadron did. But the war must come first, he resolved silently. "No," he said. "We would never give up that fast or that easily."

"They will," said Dale firmly. "Don't argue with me, Sam. Look where you are. You're on a Luftwaffe starship. I assure you, the United States gives up on the war."

"I wasn't arguing that," he said, trying to hold off the regret in his voice.

The tenderness in her voice resumed. "Sam, your own effort in the war was profound. Don't ever forget that. But that was only one part of it. There is so much more to this war than the Italian campaign. The invasion of France ends on the beaches. That will be the major catastrophe that turns the war. Thousands are killed with nothing to show for it."

"We've lost battles before," he said, thinking of the initial setback in Cassino.

"Not like this. Not with such obvious incompetence. They should have known this was going to happen. There will be a practice invasion next month on a small British island. The defenses for the exercise are inadequate. A thousand men will be killed when German ships come upon them. Your politicians keep those deaths a secret until after the war.

"Then more horrors in the days leading up to the invasion. English and American forces are already conducting massive bombings on the French coast right now. Tens of thousands of innocent French civilians will be killed — including women and children. And when the actual invasion begins, more bombs miss their targets. Parachute troops land in the wrong place. Thousands die on the beaches. The very first wave of soldiers is wiped out almost entirely — nearly every man dead. But the generals continue sending in more men, even when the weather worsens.

"All this is for what? England only started this war to prop up Poland's government when it refused to let German-speaking lands become part of Germany — which is what the people in that region wanted. Even if you thought it was important to deny them self-determination, you can't tell me it's *that* important.

"Anyway, your President Roosevelt has his stroke the next day. Vice President Henry Wallace becomes the new President while your Congress calls for hearings into the fiasco. You know they're still pointing fingers over the Pearl Harbor attack. Hitler, once again, offers to negotiate. You didn't know about the earlier peace offer last year; they kept that from you. It will be leaked to the press, but too late, and relegated to the back pages.

"President Wallace makes a show of refusing the new peace offer. But a few days later, just one week after the failed invasion, London is showered with unmanned flying bombs called the V-1. The English people will then regret what that warmonger Churchill led them into. In America, the ice breaks when mothers of soldiers meet with President Wallace. Adolf Hitler, again, offers an honorable peace, and that will be the end of the alliance against the Germans."

McHenry fell silent again, brooding over her words. It wasn't just the mistakes in battle. That was normal throughout the war. But he detested her detached attitude. *Your President Roosevelt*, she had said. The words hurt, grating on his sense of patriotism. He couldn't help but think that he should have been *her* President Roosevelt, too. Her voice sounded so much like an American, particularly since he had resisted looking at her SS uniform. Staring at the wide view screen, he could see Europe, Great Britain and the east coast of the United States. The world looked so much smaller from here, and the United States so vulnerable.

He turned his thoughts to the expected invasion. It was a subject he had been well aware of. Newspapers were often talking about it. His squadron was to play no direct part in it, as they'd have their hands full in Italy. Yet, he felt a pang of regret that his squadron would not be covering the men on the ground in France. He wanted to be there himself, all the more if it was going to fail when one more set of wings might make the difference. But Dale would have none of it.

"The European Civil War was over in weeks," she said. "The people had tired of it. Even before the invasion attempt, four out of ten Americans admitted in a poll that they didn't have a clear idea what the war was really about. Unlike the thousand soldiers killed in the practice run, the politicians will not be able to cover up this failure. Adolf Hitler will propose a way out, and the people will finally listen. Its resolution saved hundreds of thousands — maybe even millions — who might have been killed if the war continued. Hitler's peace overture was a humanitarian gesture appreciated by the entire world."

McHenry wanted to scoff at that but Dale continued: "I might even say that Hitler and Wallace had saved my own life. More of my ancestors would have been drafted, and possibly killed, if President Wallace hadn't ended this immoral war when he did. I wouldn't have been born."

"What about the Russians?," McHenry asked. "I can't see them giving up."

"They didn't want to be alone fighting Germany. It was only Roosevelt's promises of this invasion that had kept Stalin from making a separate peace. He had been waiting for the invasion since 1942. It was supposed to force Germany to face a true second front. Your Africa and Italy campaigns were a poor substitute."

After a long interval, McHenry looked up again. "And the Jews?"

"What do you mean?" she asked blankly.

"The Jews. What happens to them? Aren't they being killed off?"

She shook her head. "That was English and Bolshevik propaganda, Sam. It's true that a great many died from disease. There was a serious problem with typhus. But most were resettled as part of the peace deal. It was just as Hitler had always planned."

He was going to sneer but she cut him off. "You will see."

She didn't let him brood. "We've been sitting here too long," she said, releasing herself from the seat. She sprang up to the rail above them and grabbed on with one hand, floating in midair. "Let's go to the watch rooms. I'll show you some of the work we're doing."

He nodded and she led him back through the tube toward one of the upper decks where he would stand under gravity again.

Once he straightened up, it was obvious that she was almost a foot taller. "Why is everybody so damned tall!" he blurted out.

"Oh, you have so much to learn," she giggled. "Everyone can be tall, strong, healthy, and intelligent. There is no disease in the Reich. You will never be sick again. And we have no pockets of poverty amidst great wealth as you had in the America of your day. There is real equality here. After you get by all your old prejudices, you will love national socialism."

*

CHAPTER 9

Just as the view from *Kontrolle* had been exhilarating, the main watch room was mystifying. Much larger than *Kontrolle*, McHenry guessed it to be almost as large as a football field. On its great dome was a projection of charts and symbols. All of it was simply beyond McHenry's understanding. He dropped his eyes from the expanse above him to survey the occupants of the area. Once again he felt like a dwarf.

About fifty men and women had staffed his end of the huge chamber, and there must have been hundreds more in the distance. Most that he could see were sitting at consoles, and all wore SS uniforms. A few men and women, not focused on the activity they monitored, turned to watch Dale and McHenry enter.

Stern stepped off the center platform and barked a command in German to one of the men beside him.

"Entering with permission," said Dale.

Stern appropriated a smile. "And so you are," he said curtly. "It is good to see you here, Herr McHenry."

"Very impressive. What is this?" The meaning behind the charts and symbols wasn't intuitively obvious.

"This is our main watch room," said Stern, raising an arm. "There are also several smaller ones, each specializing in a particular aspect of the main task."

"And what, exactly, is that task?" asked McHenry.

"We are historians. We have sensors collecting and recording images of the events unfolding below. Some are on this ship, looking downward, and others are on probes positioned in orbit around the Earth. They monitor every detail so that we may have a full recording of history as it actually transpired."

"You mean, you're looking down on people?"

"Yes, we are looking at everything and everybody. Or rather, the sensors peer down, collect and interpret the information, and our rechners compile it into these quantified streams of events."

He stepped to the left and pointed up to a heavy patch of lines and symbols on one side of the dome.

"Do you see the thicker lines?" he asked.

"Yes," McHenry said, looking up to a region where many of the lines had converged, mostly green and blue with some red and white.

"Those main lines, C25, C26 and P25, are our designators for your coming invasion of France."

The topic took McHenry by surprise. His heart leapt but he tried to appear cool. "That doesn't look like the coast of France," he said.

"This is not a map," said Stern. "Or rather, it is not a geographical map. You may think of it as a map of time — of events in history." Stern's arm moved back down along one axis, "The blue and green section represents the events that have already transpired as the forces prepare the way. Some of these other lines have still not happened yet, in current time, and most of that is marked in green. But our machines have already acquired sufficient data to fill in the events we do not yet have. You see, we are making projections as to what will happen as we analyze the course of history."

"Hold just a second," said McHenry. "What do you mean, making projections? You mean, as in predictions? If you guys are from the future, don't you already know what's going to happen?"

"Not in such detail. In a battle, for example, we know which men are sent out on a particular mission, but not necessarily who shoots whom. Some of the work we are doing now will become clearer when we have all the reports."

"We don't get everything at once, Sam," Dale volunteered. "Some of this stuff is still on the satellites and we won't have that until the Luftwaffe pilots bring it back in."

"Yes," Stern acknowledged. "The satellites must be retrieved for more data to be collected. You see, those satellites cannot use radio signals, especially now that we have totally restricted transmissions."

He pointed overhead to another section of the great hall, where the entire corner was a patch of green and blue.

"Those," he said proudly, "have been completely charted. See how the intersections are spaced out in waves?"

McHenry saw the pattern and nodded.

Stern shouted a command, and the section zoomed in on a patchwork. "Those are one hundred percent mapped out. The wave pattern follows the predictions made by the formulae. There are no breaks. You see where the green merges with the blue perfectly."

"That was the entire last year," Dale said.

"Last year? How long have you people been here?"

"Six months," she replied. "But that's what's so important about the work we are doing. With the small amount of data we already have, we will be able to extrapolate backward as well as forward. We will soon have most of the next two years plotted out, as well as the last five, even without more data."

"You seem to be saying that you will be able to predict events," McHenry noted almost accusingly.

"Yes, of course," said Stern. "Taken as a whole, there are patterns and cycles to history. Some of this is already being researched in your time to study cycles in the economy. Have you ever heard about Kondratiev cycles and Elliott waves?"

"No. My field was engineering, not economics."

"You will still understand the basics," Stern continued. "Nikolai Kondratiev, a Russian, found long-term cycles to the aggregate world economy. Those cycles take decades. Ralph Nelson Elliott was, or is, rather, an American. He found patterns in shorter time periods. They were not the first, nor the last. Men were writing about economic cycles for centuries. But these are men of your time.

"There are also broader trends. You have heard, no doubt, that we have a rechner operating aboard this ship — a vast number of them, actually. But there are early primitive versions of the rechners today. In your time, presently, the British are using one with banks of radio tubes to decipher secret German codes. For a time, Americans will call them 'computers.' But even this was not the beginning. An earlier generation used mechanical relays. The next generation will use silicon, and then technology at the molecular level. It will still improve from there.

"I am not telling you all this because I think you need a lesson in early technology. My point is that technology, an important facet of society, is ever-advancing at a rate that is quantifiable. Even if I did not have records to show me who will invent a new technology, I could estimate when it will happen. Then, knowing what technology will be available, in conjunction with knowing the world economic situation at that time, I could make projections."

"But it's all still approximate," McHenry noted.

Stern smiled. "Look around, Herr McHenry. Elliott waves and Kondratiev cycles are as much a part of your era as vacuum tubes. We have moved well beyond that." He called out another command in German.

The dome returned to the scale it had shown before. McHenry studied the green and blue section and followed the lines back to the area they looked at first, C25, C26 and P25 — the invasion of France. He desperately wanted to know more about it, but dared not ask, lest he be disappointed further. "What are those red markings?" he asked.

"Those? You might call them surprises," Stern answered. "An event was unexpected when the predicted or actual wave patterns did not match our historical records precisely. We are still waiting for more data to fully comprehend these. As it comes in, those surprises are reconciled with the pattern, and change to green or blue. Most of our satellites are retrieved regularly. Some of our most sensitive ones will not be recalled until much later. In those cases, we will have to wait for that to be resolved."

"If you want my opinion, you're being just a little too careful about not using radio," said McHenry. "My people are too busy down there to be listening for what you're all up to."

"Oh, we are not afraid of being overheard down there," said Stern. "Your old equipment would not detect us. We do not need to use the old-style radio bands. It is the Grauen we have to watch for."

"You have to understand, we don't dare fight them here," said Dale, her face revealing a touch of concern. "Their history is also intertwined with ours."

Stern stepped onto his raised platform. "Correct. We must allow them to go on with their activities, whatever it was, and no matter how nefarious. There must be no distractions from us." He turned to address Dale. "*Sturmbannführer*, perhaps you should show Herr McHenry to the upper storerooms."

"Ah, yes," she said, smiling confidently again. "That is something he would like to see. With your permission, *Standartenführer*?"

"Certainly."

"*Heil Renard!*" said Dale, raising her hand.

"*Heil Renard!*" answered Stern.

Dale led the way through another set of doors, and through another long corridor. Everyone they passed in these halls wore SS uniforms.

"I guess the Luftwaffe doesn't work in this department," McHenry observed.

"They run the ship and do flight operations," Dale replied. "We're the historians."

"If you'll excuse me for saying, that doesn't sound like the SS I know about."

"And what do you really know about the SS?" she laughed. "Sam, you've got to get over your preconceptions. The SS is primarily responsible for national security. That's an important function for any society. Even the corrupt democracy of your day had its counterparts in the FBI and OSS. This is serious business. Any mistakes here would be a disaster. The Reich can't afford to leave anything to chance. The task demands the integrity and the authority of the SS. Men, women and children of the next thousand years would be at risk if we messed up. Surely, you must be able to grasp this by now."

McHenry understood her words but was not willing to give in. "A thousand years," he mused. "Isn't that how long Hitler said the Third Reich would last?"

She turned a corner and stopped before a numbered door.

"Adolf Hitler was the greatest man in history," she replied. Her voice took a more reverent tone, smoothing her Chicago edge. "But even he failed to see how powerful the vision was. The Third Reich will stand for an eternity. You can depend on that."

*

CHAPTER 10

> "We don't know when an invasion of Europe will begin, but we do know that when it does begin it will be the great test, not only of our men in the field, but of us at home."
> — *Eleanor Roosevelt, First Lady, (April 10, 1944)*

The door opened when she gave it a determined glare. "You're gonna like this," she said.

The room was full of helmeted twentieth-century SS troops, about two dozen in number. They wore the gray uniforms of the Waffen-SS, and stood rigidly at attention. Every man was about McHenry's height, with some variation. Dale was by far the tallest person in the room, and she stood out in that way.

"Heil Renard!" said the first man in the line. He was an officer in the twentieth-century uniform, clicking his heels and standing straight at attention with his right arm extended in salute.

"Heil Renard!" Dale responded, saluting with a raised hand, curtly. "Good morning, *Hauptsturmführer*. We're speaking English for Herr McHenry here. He is an American of the twentieth-century and does not speak German."

"Good morning then," the man said, speaking with a flawless American accent.

"Good morning," said McHenry, eyeing the troops. With the exception of the one who spoke, the rest were too rigid to be normal men, as though frozen in place. "May I ask what's going on?"

"I was not briefed," said the strange man.

"Nothing is going on, Herr *Hauptsturmführer*," said Dale. "This is Lieutenant Sam McHenry. He's an American pilot. I am giving him a tour of the facilities."

"Welcome, Lieutenant." The man clicked his heels again and reached out to shake McHenry's hand.

"Thanks," said McHenry. It was a firm and warm handshake.

Dale smiled deviously. "Sam," she said, "the *Hauptsturmführer* is a robot."

McHenry stepped back and let his eyes sweep the room again. "A robot?" he asked, dumbfounded, though not entirely surprised. "I just assumed *Hauptsturmführer* was another one of your SS ranks."

"Yes, *Hauptsturmführer* is an SS rank." said Dale. "It would be equivalent to a *Hauptmann* in the Luftwaffe or a Captain in the American army. But these are our SS troops."

"Does that surprise you?" asked the robot. He, or it — McHenry wasn't quite sure — had remained standing with the rigidity of a well disciplined German SS officer, but not that of a machine.

"I thought I've seen too many surprises already, but yes, I am surprised."

"Really?" The robot's expression feigned puzzlement. "But we know that twentieth-century Americans have already discussed the possibility of mechanical men."

"Maybe so, but it's different to see one." McHenry gave another look to the robot's platoon. Unlike the *Hauptsturmführer*, the rest stood stiff like mannequins. "Are you planning to invade?"

"We stand ready to follow orders, whatever they may be."

"These mechanical troops are here just as a precaution," said Dale. "It is technically a unit of *Fallschirmjäger*, the German word for paratrooper. If some kind of accident happened, like a Tiger crash, or anything that might change history, we can mobilize them to set things right again."

McHenry turned back to the robot. "Does that mean you can parachute down from orbit?"

The robot looked to Dale as though awaiting permission to reveal a secret.

"Yes," Dale answered, nodding to the robot. "It is more complicated than that." Then, after a pause, she laughed and pointed a finger down at his chest. "If you're thinking of stealing a parachute, forget it. Humans can't survive that trip with the ones that our *Fallschirmjäger* use. And you don't have access to the exits. The ship's main rechner will see to that."

"You don't leave much to chance," McHenry said, glumly.

"Sam, you ought to know by now that we leave nothing to chance."

McHenry saw she was beaming with pride. A boastful, Nazi pride. He didn't like it. He would not accept such perfection. He scanned the robot, looking for flaws.

"Why are the others so rigid?"

"They are not active," said the robot. "Their memories are blank. Mine would also be reset if I were sent to the planet's surface."

"Reset?"

"They will be given fresh instructions when needed."

McHenry's face expressed shock.

"One thing you have to realize," she interrupted, "is that we don't want them to have any more information than necessary. Their memories can be scanned by the Grauen if they're captured."

"Yes," added the robot. "I am alert now only as a backup measure. If *Göring* and her crew are disabled, I can use whatever means are available to either save or destroy the ship. But my primary function is emergency intervention. If I go to the surface, my memory will also be cleared, and given only the information I need to carry out my mission."

"And this doesn't bother you?" McHenry asked, incredulously.

"Oh, Sam!" Dale laughed. "He's a machine."

"But he is..." McHenry searched for the word, wondering what it was that separated himself from this machine. Dale kept grinning, seeming to enjoy teasing him. The robot stood at ease with himself, watching McHenry as though studying him.

And then it hit him. They were studying each other. This machine was aware of itself — aware of *himself*. It wasn't a machine at all in McHenry's mind, and yet it wasn't upset that it might have its memory cleared. "He is *aware*," McHenry finally said to Dale, and then turned to the robot. "You *know* what's going on. They shouldn't be able to just erase your memory like you're some kind of a radio."

"He's still a machine," said Dale.

The robot stood there, now grinning like Dale, but it didn't say anything. McHenry couldn't think of it as a machine. He wondered what it was thinking.

"There's no use in arguing with you people," he conceded. Neither Dale nor the robot said anything for the moment. He had no hope of knowing what the robot was thinking, but Dale's smirk led him to assume she was relishing this victory. She looked every bit the victor, towering over him with her imposing physique, and flashing her perfect white teeth. The word *arrogance* crossed his mind and it stuck. He had thought this about her before, and about many of these people, particularly Mtubo the SS, but the word fit her in this moment in time.

He finally understood. These people hadn't merely advanced their physical bodies. Their brains must have been advanced as well, presumably by Nazi science. And then there was the all-too-easily forgotten fact that she was old enough to be a great-great grandmother. There was no telling how much smarter they were. Her arrogance may have been justified—

No, he was wrong. It wasn't arrogance at all. It was *confidence*. The word fit all of them like the last piece in a jigsaw puzzle. He never had a chance to overpower them, and he now knew that outsmarting them was out of the question. That realization was like a stake into his heart.

"Don't feel bad," said Dale, her grin fading into an expression of concern. "You're learning."

"Not fast enough," he replied.

"You have all the time in the world."

He wanted to contradict her. He did not have all the time in the world. He had a war to fight.

"Let's have lunch," she said. "That's one thing I'm sure you'll enjoy."

CHAPTER 11

SCHOOLS TO FINANCE P-51 MUSTANG

In February, boys and girls of the schools of
Washington County financed the purchase of a Flying
Ambulance, buying $182,000 worth of War Bonds and
Stamps. The goal was $110,000. Bond and stamp
sales in March totaled $75,000. This month, April, the
schools of the county are being asked to finance a
P-51 Mustang Fighter, which has the "highest ceiling
and the highest speed of any fighter in existence."
These fighters cost $75,000 each.
— *The Washington Reporter, (April 10, 1944)*

The SS officers' mess was not at all like the Luftwaffe pilots' mess. The food could be the same, but they sat in an alcove rather than a large open room. McHenry sat across from Dale at the small table that could seat six at most.

He was also surprised that he could ask for any food he wanted. "Why do the Luftwaffe pilots all eat the same thing?" he asked.

"Tradition," Dale explained. "It goes back to the early days of space flight when everyone ate together. It's like a social exercise to them. It probably helps to pass the time when they're in transit. But we're on a different schedule. And we don't have the same traditions. Now, what would you like?"

"What are my options?"

"The rechner can serve anything you want."

"Steak," he answered. "With potatoes, greens, gravy and a cola."

Almost immediately, the food emerged from the dispenser in the center of the table. But he was less surprised than he would have been the previous day.

Dale ordered something in German, which looked like a salad.

"Where is everybody else?" he asked.

She smiled. "Most of us eat at our stations, but there are also several break rooms where we can relax."

"You guys must work a lot."

"We do."

He was still surprised. "Every single day? All you people do is work from morning to night?"

Now she was surprised. She looked in his eyes. "Don't you know? We work twenty-four hours a day — with breaks, of course."

McHenry eyed her warily. "You don't sleep?"

"Not since we were teenagers. Nobody does unless there is a special medical need."

He looked down at his steak and wondered if it was real, then cursed himself for even thinking that it could be.

"Don't fret so," said Dale, consoling him. "Hasn't your sleeping gone well?"

"Only too well," he said, very conscious of the odd way she said that. He continued eating, no longer caring whether it could ever have been real. "Just tell me one thing..."

"What's that?"

He set his fork down and straightened up. "If I'm the only one who sleeps around here, then why does everyone need their own quarters?"

She raised an eyebrow. "We don't."

"But what about those other rooms near...?" His voice trailed off, suddenly realizing he may know the answer.

She picked up his meaning. "The other rooms near yours? Those are for the other people we will be picking up — more people from the past. You are only the first where we were successful."

McHenry perked up. "Anybody I know?"

"No. If there were, I probably would have told you already. We check all the backgrounds for convergences. There are only three other Americans. The first is a scientist who will be killed in an industrial accident. But that's a difficult one. We may not be able to do it. And we don't get him for another six months anyway."

"When do you get the next one?"

"Next week," she said. "And it's an easy one. He'll be in the water, just like you were."

"I see," he said. "Another downed pilot?"

"No. He's an Italian naval officer. His ship is going to sink."

McHenry pondered the image in his mind. "Why just one? Won't there be a whole ship full of people you can rescue?"

"I wish it were so," she replied. "It just isn't that simple. There are a lot of variables we need to consider. He's the only one we can safely recover."

"I see," he said again. Then he got back to his steak and wondered if the day would come when he doesn't need to sleep.

*

McHenry spotted Vinson and Barr having coffee in the pilots' mess.

"I see the prince is back from his tour," chided Barr. McHenry wondered momentarily about that mustache, and what he needed to do in order to grow one, although it certainly wouldn't be a Hitler mustache. He had already accepted Otto Barr as being both black and a Luftwaffe pilot.

"Did you see very much?" asked Vinson.

McHenry nodded and took a seat. "The main watch room."

Barr and Vinson raised their eyebrows in unison.

"You know the watch room?" McHenry asked, seeing their blank expressions.

"We do not go into that part of the ship," said Barr. "The SS has their job to do, and we have ours."

"So I've been told. Aren't you curious?"

Vinson looked like he was looking for an answer, but Barr kept the point. "Perhaps a little, but we understand the security considerations. As pilots, we are more susceptible to capture than most people aboard the ship. They cannot tell us more than we need to know for the mission."

"I understand that all too well," McHenry replied. "But what about Dale? She goes on flights."

Barr nodded. "We do take an SS officer on most missions. They use a side-panel to access separate information. But I am certain they are told only as much as they need to know to accomplish their tasks. Those who know more don't leave the *Göring*. It is for the best. As a combat pilot yourself, you know that ours is a profession that demands we focus on the task at hand."

"Coffee?" Vinson offered, interrupting before McHenry could respond.

"I have a better idea," Barr interjected. "We should take our coffee inside the Tiger, so McHenry can continue his flight training."

McHenry's eyes beamed. "Thanks!"

To his surprise, the men left their unfinished coffee cups on the table when they filed out the door toward the hangar section.

"You are getting better at this," Vinson noted as they entered the zero-gee section and floated up the ladder.

"I can get used to it." He wondered how they could drink coffee without gravity, but didn't want to say anything that would delay a flight lesson.

All three Tigers were parked in the hangar. Two men were working near one of the ships. It looked to McHenry as though they were inspecting its nose. Barr, the senior pilot there, took the lead toward the closest of the other two. He entered first. Vinson held out his hand, motioning for McHenry to follow Barr.

This looked like the same Tiger, although McHenry couldn't be sure. He would find out later that they always looked exactly the same on the inside unless one was specially configured for a particular mission or maintenance procedure. There were never tears in the fabric, cracks in the glass, or other imperfections by which McHenry could learn to recognize each ship.

Barr had taken a position behind the two front seats. McHenry took the right seat, flinching a bit when the automatic harness grabbed onto him.

"How do you like your coffee?" Barr asked.

"Cream and sugar."

Vinson explained as Barr ordered coffees for the three of them, "The Tiger's rechner is cleared whenever it goes out on a mission. It cannot always remember how we like our coffee."

"You mean the one on *Göring* does?" McHenry thought about how robots were erased before a mission, and understood this must be common military practice. Security was like a science to the Reich.

"Yes," answered Vinson. "Back on Earth, all the machines communicate with each other. You will be able to drink coffee in Berlin and the machines in Brazil will know how you like it."

McHenry suddenly stiffened. He didn't want to go to Berlin. Then he wondered whether his lesson would begin after the coffee. The dome was still just a blank test pattern. Neither Barr nor Vinson seemed in a hurry. "What you're really saying," he mused, "is that the rechner on *Göring* is always listening to every word we say. And we have privacy on the Tigers."

"Don't make it sound nefarious," Vinson said uneasily. "It is not as though we are planning a mutiny. We are just more at ease here."

"Especially since the main rechner on *Göring* is now running an SS program," added Barr. He handed out sealed containers with a straw on one end. The coffee was just as good as inside *Göring*.

Vinson rotated his seat toward McHenry and Barr — an act McHenry hadn't thought the seat was capable of. He pushed harder on one foot, and his seat swiveled too.

"Did you have coffee with the SS?" asked Barr.

"No, I had a cola with lunch."

Barr leaned back casually. "Did you eat in the watch room?"

"We ate in a small separate room. I was only in the watch room for a few minutes."

"What was it like?" asked Vinson.

"Big. Tremendously huge. It was a little bit like a theater except that these motion picture screens were all over the place. The ceiling had a large one of these." McHenry pointed toward the dome. "It was much bigger than in *Kontrolle*."

"Did you see what was on the screens?" asked Barr.

"I only saw the lines overhead, and it was covered with charts of some type. They told me it represented history. Everything was leading toward the planned invasion. You guys probably understand it a lot better than me."

"We can make guesses," said Barr. "But this is out of our expertise. The work is tightly classified for good reason, and you should consider yourself lucky to have seen any of it. They are trying to make a good impression on you. Take advantage of your good fortune. See and learn as much as you can."

"Did you spend much time with *Sturmbannführer* Dale?" asked Vinson hesitantly.

It took a second for McHenry to figure out that he meant Kathy Dale. He couldn't resist a slight smile. "She gave me the tour," he said. "We had lunch afterward. Interesting woman." He half-expected Barr to jibe Vinson again.

"You will probably be seeing a lot of her," Barr noted. "I think the SS will want to take an active part introducing you to our time."

The word *indoctrination* flashed into McHenry's mind. He bristled.

Vinson seemed to sense that. "You are in good hands. She was a teacher before returning to the SS." He set his coffee cup onto a clasp in the seat and looked to Barr.

"Time for your lesson," said Barr. "Orbital navigation."

*

CHAPTER 12

"When the President is ill Roosevelt-haters turn pollyanna and dish out oodles of counterfeit sympathy. They whimper that he works hard and carries tremendous responsibilities... They seem to forget that one reason the President gets sick is that he is continually hounded, annoyed and obstructed by their low-blow attacks."
— *Walter Winchell, newspaper and radio commentator, (April 16, 1944)*

Sunday, April 16, 1944

McHenry would see Dale almost every day for breakfast or lunch.

She met him at the border to the SS section, as she had done on previous occasions. It was hardly necessary. The rechner controlled access throughout the ship, and he had learned quickly that the doors only opened when he was authorized to proceed. Having established that the future would breed a superior humanity, he imagined that she might have thought he wasn't capable of remembering the path as all the corridors looked alike here. He hoped this was the case. The idea of proving her wrong pleased him so much.

"We will have to have a quick breakfast this morning," she said as they walked through the corridors. "I'm sure you know that we're intercepting the Italian today."

"You haven't told me whether you'll be going along."

"Not this time. Someone else is assigned to that one."

"I noticed Adolf Vinson isn't going either." He couldn't help watching her for a reaction to hearing the name, but she didn't show one.

"No, the pilot is named Bamberg. I'm sure you know him already. That reminds me, how are your flight lessons going?"

"Great," he replied. That was his first heartfelt response to her in a long time. He realized that there were few in any of their conversations. She didn't seem to understand that he still resented that swastika on her arm.

They entered the SS officers' mess. He sat down after she did, and then they ordered breakfast.

"I understand you're becoming a pretty good Tiger pilot."

"It's still just in simulator mode — or *Flug Spiel*," he answered. "I'm still waiting for someone to authorize a trip for me."

"You know that will have to wait until we return to our time." She watched him for a moment as he took a spoonful of grits. "But I can see you're picking up some German."

"Mostly what I see on the Tiger visuals. It's not so easy with everybody speaking English when I'm around."

"Everyone wants you to feel comfortable," she said. She had stopped eating and was still watching him intently. "You know, there are other subjects that you can study while we're here."

"Such as?"

"Something other than space flight," she said. "There is so much to learn, and all you've done is practice flying."

"I'm a pilot," he said. "That's what I do."

"Anything to pass the time?"

"What else do you expect me to do?" he asked. He noticed that she kept watching him. Her scrutiny made him suddenly conscious of how small he was.

"You could study the Reich, and its rich history. You have one thousand years of history to learn about."

"I've seen its history close up, remember?" he sneered.

"You know that's not what I mean," she responded. "But I should say that I am astonished that you haven't tried looking up your friends. You can even look for their future descendants. You know that the rechner is capable telling you everything you want to know."

"Not quite everything," he replied, knowing full well it was a pointless response.

"Everything you need to know," she said, rephrasing the point more accurately.

He knew what she was driving at, and that she was right. He had deliberately avoided trying to find out what happens to his friends and family. He would spend his days in the hangar or the pilots' mess. Every night he went to bed staring out the fake window above the world, allowing its distance to shield him from the question that some of his friends may be dying in the clouds far below.

He also knew that his new Luftwaffe friends were happy to let him avoid this truth. Why was she, a woman with a swastika on her arm, trying to make him confront it?

"It's not like I don't think about it," he finally said, staring at his food. "I think about my friends every day. But as you are so fond of saying, there's nothing I can do about it. I've got to work this out on my own."

"That's all right," she consoled him. "There will always be time for that in the future. You might feel better if you look at the future first. That's why I suggest that you learn more about the Reich. Adolf Hitler was only the beginning. You have so much more to see. Get yourself settled into your new life. Then when you're ready to reflect on the past, you will have a firm footing in your new life to hold onto.

"We understand you face some difficulties," she continued. "Everyone here is thinking of you."

*

The rechner played his favorite song when McHenry returned to his room that night. He marveled at the quality of the recording, which made it sound as though the musician was in the room. But his favorite song reminded him of home. His thoughts came back to his friends. Where were they now? And which ones would not survive the war?

"Rechner!" he called. "Show me a list of the pilots from the U.S. Army Air Force 99th Fighter Squadron who died." That was the question he dared not ask, and now it came out without his even thinking.

The result was devastating. The entire wall filled with names. McHenry stared in shock. He could hardly read the list, his eyes filling with tears. There were so many, he dared not look for the most familiar names.

"How did they all die?" he asked, his voice a mere whisper.

The machine responded without emotion: "Seventy-nine percent attributed to illness or other natural causes. Five percent accidental deaths. Fifteen percent killed during war-time service. One percent list no record of death."

The dry recital made no sense. Slowly, he realized the error. "Do you mean that most of these men died of old age?"

"Yes. Fifty-seven percent died of old age."

He sank back into his chair, relieved but angry. Of course, he thought, everybody he knew would be dead after one thousand years. He wondered whether the machine could have foreseen his reaction, and asked himself why it would allow him to make such a heart-rending mistake.

Correcting the error would have been easy now. All he needed to do was ask for a list of those killed in combat. But he wasn't ready for that now.

"Rechner, show me the *Fenster* again." The Earth appeared and the names were gone. The music kept playing.

He thought he would feel better. He didn't. He wondered what Parker would do, and then he wondered whether Parker survives the war. That was something that couldn't wait. He needed to know now.

"Tell me what happens to Captain Joseph Parker," he ordered, his voice firm. "Same unit. What happens to him?"

He knew the answer even before the machine spoke.

"Captain Joseph Charles Parker was killed in combat during war-time service."

*

McHenry decided to miss breakfast with the pilots that morning. Most of the pilots would be in training anyway, and yesterday's Tiger mission wouldn't return until mid-afternoon. It seemed the perfect opportunity to sulk.

A chime sounded. It was a familiar sound, but he couldn't remember where he heard it before. Looking around his room, he saw a message displayed on the window.

SS-SF Kathy Dale

"Rechner, what was that?" he called.

"*Sturmbannführer* Dale is waiting at your door."

"Then, that's a doorbell?" he asked absentmindedly, getting to his feet.

"Yes."

He straightened himself, checking that his shirt was taut. He was still not used to the fact that his clothing seemed to know when to relax and when to firm up.

"Well, open the door."

"I was worried about you," said Dale as she stepped inside. "I heard that you missed breakfast this morning, and all I could think about was the conversation we had yesterday. Please tell me you didn't get some bad news."

McHenry studied her face. She seemed genuinely concerned, but that swastika on her arm was so ugly to him. Especially now. He almost wanted to blame her for Parker's impending death.

"My flight leader is going to die," he said. "He's my best friend."

"Oh Sam, I'm so sorry." Dale took a seat that seemed to slide out of the wall and tapped his chair, beckoning him to sit beside her. This timeless gesture hadn't changed in a thousand years.

"Sam," she continued softly. "Let me tell you something I really only understood a few years ago. As you know, I am a lot older than you are. Much, much older. One of the differences with our immortality is that people can live for many years without ever losing anyone they love. You have lived a very short life and have already seen death many times."

"That doesn't make it any easier," said McHenry, almost instantly regretting the sour tone. He could see tears forming in her eyes.

"Sam, I lost two of my grandchildren once."

Those words startled him. He remembered, again, she wasn't the young woman she appeared to be.

"It was an accident," she explained. "They could have easily survived if they had been on Earth, or on any starship, or any one of a dozen planets. You know that doctors can repair anything. But they died on another world far from here."

"I'm sorry," said McHenry. It was the first time he saw her in despair, having shed her cloak of Nazi pride.

"I have five children, and now six other grandchildren. That didn't make it any easier for me. I lived the first hundred years of my life without ever losing anyone who was truly close to me. Not an uncle; not a grandfather; and certainly not a child. This happened fifteen years ago, and I'm still not over it."

"I don't mean to take away from your loss."

"That's okay, Sam. You see, I do understand. You won't ever forget your friends and family either."

"He just meant a lot to me, that's all," said McHenry. "He's the one who stood by my side whenever I had problems, and now I won't be there for him. He was the last man I saw before I..."

He sunk his head down and closed his eyes. He had wanted to show strength but gave in to the emotion.

Dale waited a moment before she spoke. "This war was such a terrible thing. I look at the casualty rates every day in my work. I need these numbers for our history equations. But I'm still a human being. I just can't get out of my mind that every one of those men had somebody who cared about them. I have to keep telling myself that the war will end. Sam, the war will end."

CHAPTER 13

"There are today hundreds of thousands of British soldiers who will cease to live during the attempt to invade Western Europe. They are prepared to sacrifice their lives, but for what? For their country? Demonstrably not! Britain has only the stark prospect of poverty before her. For the rights of small nations? Certainly not. What British politician wants to hear of Poland today? For what, then, are these men to die? They are to die for the Jewish policy of Stalin and Roosevelt. If there is any other purpose to their sacrifice, I challenge Mr. Churchill to tell them what it is."
— *William Joyce, Nazi propaganda broadcaster, (April 17, 1944)*

Monday, April 17, 1944

"We missed you at breakfast this morning," said Vinson. He and Dr. Evers were waiting at the hangar in the same corner that McHenry would go to whenever there wasn't a Tiger available for him to board.

"I needed to be alone," McHenry answered curtly. He looked across at the one empty moor, one Tiger evidently overdue.

"They're not back yet," explained Vinson. "There could be many reasons for this. He can't leave the water until the horizon is clear."

"How late are they now?"

"Two hours," said Evers.

McHenry was a little disappointed, having looked forward to meeting the Italian. Then a thought occurred to him. "Do any of you guys speak Italian?"

"Of course," said Vinson.

"Everybody does," the doctor added. "Every Hitler Youth can speak at least twenty languages."

"Oh." McHenry regretted the question. "I guess that explains how everyone here can speak English."

"Do you speak no other languages?" asked Vinson.

"I'm fluent in French. I'm afraid that's it."

Evers put his hand on McHenry's shoulder. "The time will come when you will speak twenty languages too. They will put you through treatments that will make it easier."

"Medical treatments?"

"Yes. After three months in Berlin, you will be a new man."

McHenry wasn't sure what to make of having his brain tampered with. The three held onto the railing, watching two technicians exit the second Tiger.

"Barr is in that one with an SS officer," noted Vinson. "They are ready to launch if we need a quick action."

A lineman floated out from the Line Office and shouted across the hangar, "*Jetzt!*" Then he turned to the corner. "Now!" McHenry was by now familiar with the routine, knew what the word meant, and imagined the man just repeated the word in English to be cordial. The Tiger was about to enter the inner seal of the ship.

A horn sounded a minute later. The inner doors opened just barely wide enough to allow the Tiger to float through, with the huge sensor-evading net retracting behind it. The doors closed quickly as the mooring arm carried it through the doors. McHenry remained very still. He was trying to sense for any breeze, or any change in pressure he thought should accompany the transition through the doors. Nothing was perceptible, and that heightened his appreciation for the technology at work here.

Evers leaned forward. "The main cargo hatch should have opened by now."

"What's wrong?" asked McHenry.

"Our new visitor will be in a life-support container. That is, if he made it."

The new visitor didn't make it. An SS man left the Tiger, beckoning Evers to follow for debrief. Vinson nodded to McHenry, and the two made their way into the Tiger.

Bamberg was still sitting inside, completing his post-flight inspection. "It was awful," he told them, speaking slowly. "There were one hundred and fifty-five men alive in the water. One hundred and fifty-five! But ours was dying. One of his comrades stayed with him, trying to save him. We kept thinking, 'come on man! Let him drown so we can pick him up!' But his friend stayed by him even as they drifted away from the others."

McHenry was touched, as apparently were both Vinson and Bamberg. The story reminded him of his friends who stayed with him when his engine cut out. He now regretted the loss of the Italian even more.

Bamberg sighed. "Hamilton said we could have killed that man if he was going to die anyway, but we didn't know who he was until it was too late. Ours died first. His friend died after an hour."

"Couldn't you get the friend?" asked McHenry.

"I know, I know," agreed Bamberg, his eyes widening. "I was thinking this, too. The SS has this all planned out mathematically. I thought it could be different once we know for a fact that they die together. I mean we can see this right here. What do we have an SS man along for if not to make decisions on the spot? But this is apparently not so."

"This is a lot more complicated than I thought," noted Vinson.

Bamberg glanced behind them and then lowered his voice. "Hamilton is on eggshells because he is looking for a promotion. I do not believe it is any more complicated than that."

*

McHenry went to his room that night thinking about the Italian officer he would never get to meet, and the man's friend who died alongside him. He didn't know whether the man could have spoken English. The man might even have been a racist. But he was certain they could have reached a common bond, especially here. It would have been nice to have another friend here in the same predicament as he. Then he saw the opportunity.

"Rechner! Tell me, where and when does Joseph Parker get killed?"

"Joseph Parker is lost and presumed killed in the Tyrrhenian Sea on 28, April, 1944."

McHenry stood, unable to contain his glee. It would have been depressing news at any other time, but now there was hope. He jumped to the door and ran toward the ladder.

He found Vinson working alone inside one of the Tigers, testing the equipment and using a tablet-like device called a *Klemmbrett* — which literally means *clipboard*, although these do so much more. He set down the tablet when McHenry came aboard.

"I need to tell you about some bad news I learned last night," McHenry announced. "My best friend from my squadron is going to die."

"That is truly awful," said Vinson.

"But there's some good news too, or at least there might be. The rechner says he will be lost in the sea, just like I was."

Vinson's expression brightened. "I see what you mean, and that would be great if he can make it! How much time do we have?"

"Until the end of April. Is that enough?"

"There is only one way to find out," said Vinson as he shut down the equipment. "We must see *Oberst* Volker immediately."

McHenry understood chain of command as well as anyone. The pair located Bamberg, Vinson's superior, and explained the story. He then called the *Kommandant* for an immediate meeting. The three proceeded to her office adjoining *Kontrolle*. Mtubo was standing beside Volker, and they listened to McHenry together. Mtubo remained impassive but the *Kommandant* eagerly followed the story.

"Ma'am, I realize I'm asking for a lot, but you've got an empty bunk here, and this should be a piece of cake. Vinson tells me that not having an exact location is not a problem."

"No, that is not a problem," said the *Kommandant*. "It is too early to be calling this cake but I do like the idea very much. It would give the crew something new to look forward to. You must understand there are no guarantees."

Mtubo looked more wary and less enthusiastic. "Indeed. Some of our people will enjoy the diversion. We will give it our best effort, even if we have to take another name off the list. No guarantees. Time travel is a risk to all the people of the Reich. We cannot put them in jeopardy."

"I understand that," said McHenry.

Volker turned to the window, looking out across the stars for a long moment before she turned back to him. "You're a soldier, Herr McHenry. Have you read Clausewitz?"

"Yes."

"Among his many insights, he wrote that all war supposes human weakness, and against that it is directed."

McHenry nodded, unsure what her point was.

"Human weakness," she repeated. "You will come to find out that we consider that dictum constantly in our war against the Grauen, but in a way that General Clausewitz could never imagine. You see, the Grauen do not think the way that we do. We do not know that their weaknesses are anything like ours. We are constantly having to second guess ourselves. But in so doing, sometimes it is best to remind ourselves that our weaknesses are what make us human, and that is sometimes a thing to be cherished. Herr McHenry, I cannot promise you that we will be able to rescue your brother in arms. The SS will study the conditions. You will have to respect their findings, whatever they may be. But I can promise you that if it can be done, we will put resources into it."

*

CHAPTER 14

GOERING PEACE MOVE

The Press association today quoted reports from an unidentified source that Reichsmarschall Hermann Goering is "likely" to go to Madrid for a conference with General Francisco Franco, with the idea of trying to arrange a compromise peace between Germany and Great Britain. The Press association's diplomatic correspondent, Frank King, said the Spanish press has been advocating a compromise recently on the theory that Franco has an "obvious interest in Germany's future."

— *British United Press, (April 18, 1944)*

Tuesday, April 18, 1944

McHenry met the pilots early for breakfast the next morning. The cafeteria was busy, with a crowd standing around the first table.

"Morning!" one of the Luftwaffe officers greeted McHenry.

"McHenry!" shouted Bamberg. "Come here! We have been waiting for you."

The table had a map on it, projected by the omnipresent rechner. It seemed as though every table on the ship was able to perform this function, one that McHenry had found a convenient study tool. He wished he had had one on his P-40. "Where is this?" he asked.

"Don't you recognize it?" asked Barr, laughing. "This is where you died."

"Yes," he answered after referencing the shore on the southwest end. "Just off the coast of Italy."

Barr put his finger on the grid. "This is where you went down." Then he moved his finger to another spot, one that McHenry guessed would be about fifty miles away. "And this is where your friend goes down."

"It's just a rough estimate," added Bamberg. "Your position was logged by a ship in the area. Your friend's position had to be estimated more crudely."

"But you've got it close enough for a recovery?" asked McHenry hesitantly.

"More than enough," replied Bamberg. "An after action review tells that it was a controlled crash. He could survive if we get to him."

"It is even better than that," said Barr. "We checked the satellite retrieval schedule. There is already a mission that morning. Your friend could not pick a better time for this to happen."

"I can't thank you guys enough," said McHenry. He studied the approach markers on the map. The words on its legend were German, most of the terms already familiar to McHenry, but the text at the center was in English. They were clearly intended for his benefit: *Rescue of Joseph Parker.* McHenry worked to restrain his emotions.

Bamberg stepped back. "Do not be too excited," he said. "Let's hold any celebration until the SS gives their approval."

That word of caution stifled McHenry's joy. The loss of the Italian weighed heavily on his mind. But a different emotion crept in as he felt he was truly among friends. He slowly swept his gaze toward everyone in the room to acknowledge them. "I want you all to know how much I really appreciate this. Even if they say no, I'll still be grateful to you all."

*

"This would be a morale booster," said Dale, after Mtubo concluded his instructions to the staff of the analysis office. She had listened to his warnings and agreed with the cautions, but so much wanted the rescue to be possible.

"Yes," agreed Mtubo. "Having two men who know each other would add to the propaganda value of the mission, particularly two

Americaners who suffered under democracy. Regardless, I should remind everyone that propaganda is not our function. We have a lot more work to do."

He waited a moment for any more comments.

"*Jawohl!*" agreed Rodriguez, the shift leader standing at attention beside Mtubo. "You may count on us, *Herr Oberführer.*"

"*Heil Renard!*" he said. The small group echoed the phrase. They relaxed only after he left the room.

Dale rushed to her console and searched for Parker's last mission. A collection of symbols and charts appeared on the display, terminating with his presumptive death only a few weeks hence. She scanned the pages back to McHenry's death. Even as passionless numbers and symbols, the impact of his loss was perceptible.

"Strange," observed Rodriguez, who had slid her chair beside Dale's station. "Two friends dying so close together."

"The symmetry alone is intriguing," said Dale. "Fate can paint such a pretty picture."

"We've been away too long," said Rodriguez.

The two watched the numbers as they paged back and forth. In just two minutes, they knew a lot about where the man had been, his impact on aggregate world history, and yet nothing about the man's soul. That would take meeting the man in the flesh.

"Hold everything," called a voice nearby. "You all better take a quick look at the color of that stream."

Dale switched back to the top. "*Scheiss!*" she gasped.

*

After spending his morning at the hangar, McHenry had to run to avoid being late for lunch with Dale. She was waiting for him in the small SS officers' mess. They were often alone for these sessions. McHenry was certain they were planned for his indoctrination. That made sense to him, and he always intended that it end as a failure for her in this regard.

"You know you've got everybody excited," she said.

97

McHenry smiled. "Oh really? Does that mean I have SS approval?"

"Sam, it's far too early to know. The analysts have a lot of work to do first. But of course you know that I approve. Even if it fails, or even if the analysts decide they must reject it, I hope you'll keep thinking this way. You've done everything you could. You should now understand that we are doing everything we can."

He tried not to let his disappointment show, determined to be firm but careful. He thought about what to say next while they ordered lunch.

"How long does it take for them to figure this out?" he finally asked.

Dale stirred her soup with the spoon as she talked. "That varies. Sometimes they know right away, and sometimes they need to wait until we have more information. I think we're going to have to wait until the next round of satellites comes in."

McHenry knotted his brow. "What makes it so different from my case?"

"A lot of the Luftwaffe people seem to think we just need to ensure that nobody sees us. But there's so much more. We can't leave any footprints either —literally or figuratively — and we need to make sure that whatever footprints would be made will still be made. When you went down, your body was dragged down with your plane. The tides weren't going to take it to the shore, nor was it going to be discovered twenty years later."

"I understand," he answered. He wanted to argue, and this time it was not for the sake of resisting. He wanted to argue a case for the sake of his friend. He also wanted to know what was going on.

"I noticed that they've sent more missions this morning. Two of the Tigers are gone."

"There is a full flight schedule now."

"You're not on it?"

"No," she said awkwardly. "I was taken off flight-status to work on a project." She looked down at his food. "Why do you eat steak every day?"

He wondered if she was trying to change the subject. "Because I like it."

"But every day?"

"Look," he said. "The place I come from, and the time that I come from, we couldn't afford to have steak every day. And when we did have it, it was never as good as this. So I'm going to enjoy this until I get tired of it."

She smiled in her enigmatic way. That always bothered him.

"Is there something wrong with that?" he asked.

"No," she laughed. "It's just interesting. You see, we don't have the same scarcity of resources that you grew up with. It probably takes as much energy to produce that steak as it would to make beans. I don't think anybody living today — I mean in my time — ever had to think about food the same way that you did."

He looked at his plate. "How much energy did it take to make this?"

"I don't know. You could ask the rechner but I doubt it would mean anything to you."

He wanted to argue that point. He was educated as an engineer, after all, and he had spent the last few days studying the quantities of energy — both minute and extreme — produced and managed by the Tigers. He understood that just fine. But he also understood her deeper meaning. He grew up in the Depression years. Food didn't just grow on trees without an enormous amount of work. At least, it didn't in his day.

"I guess I had been in the Army so long," he said. "I just assumed these were military rations. Do civilians eat this well? Rich or poor?"

"This is national socialism," she said. "We don't have any poor. Even in the early Hitler times, the total elimination of poverty was what made Germany a model for the rest of the world. It was the first country in Europe to overcome the class struggle."

"I'm having trouble understanding your hatred of communists," he said. "You sure speak like one."

"Not at all!" she shot back. "We are neither capitalists nor Bolscheviks. Adolf Hitler said the nation does not live for the sake of the economic system, and the economic system does not exist for the sake of capital. The state shut down the small corporations, and formed boards to guard against abuses by the large ones. But unlike the Bolscheviks, we have always allowed small businesses, like shopkeepers, as long as they do not to use their property against the interests of others."

McHenry sighed. It still sounded close enough. He didn't want to debate politics again, but he knew this was an inevitable part of her indoctrination attempts.

"Okay," he admitted. "I remember reading an article by W. E. B. Du Bois, who visited Berlin during the Olympics. Germany came out of the Depression early. Some people envied that."

"Yes, you understand!" she said. Her eyes brightened.

He wasn't going to let her have that. "I also remember that Hitler didn't want to shake hands with Jesse Owens."

Dale frowned and shook her head. "That was American propaganda. Adolf Hitler didn't shake hands with any foreign athletes. It was your President Roosevelt who did not shake hands with Owens after he'd returned from the Germany."

McHenry held back any defense of his president. He knew she was right. 1936 was an election year. Roosevelt needed to hold the white vote.

"You've got an answer for everything, don't you?"

"Not everything," she replied. "We as individuals are not perfect. The Reich had suffered through many struggles, and not just the one we are witnessing here today. We made mistakes along the way. But most of those mistakes were simply the best option that was available at that time."

He wondered what she could be leading up to. It sounded like the preface to an apology. "I don't take your meaning," he said.

She kept her eyes focused on his. "I don't discount that Adolf Hitler was a champion for the Aryan people. As you know quite well, that was the character of the times. Most people were like that back then. Homo sapiens, just a few steps up from the apes. Nonetheless, you should know that when Du Bois visited Germany in 1936 he didn't need to go looking for a special hotel that accepted black men."

McHenry didn't really know for sure whether that was true. It all sounded like more propaganda.

"Sam," she continued, "you need to look beyond all that and see Adolf Hitler for the state that he created. They took the politics out of the system. An entire nation doesn't have to stop every four years just to bicker about which set of oligarchs run the system. Everywhere you look in America, you see clever advertisements with politicians slandering opponents with half-truths and outright lies. They spend an enormous amount of money on this. It's a terrible waste of resources. And most of your politicians don't care about the people nearly as much as they care about getting elected again the next time. I know that democracy sounds like a wonderful concept but none of its promises are true. Now in the Reich, we all have a nation where leaders are not chosen by who has the best advertisements. Our leaders aren't bought. They can devote all their energies to the people of the Reich."

"I still believe that democracy is too important a thing not to fight for it."

"Whose democracy were you fighting for? Let me quote an American from your day." She shifted in her seat slightly. Her voice took a colder pitch. "*Once again, may I inform you that Great Britain is not a democracy in any sense of the word. It is an empire of 486 million persons who are ruled, regulated, and in some instances exploited by the members of the British Parliament elected to office by no more than 45 million residents of England and Scotland.*"

McHenry understood that Dale was reciting a passage from memory, but he didn't recognize the source.

She continued, "*Nor is France a democracy. It, too, is an empire boasting of more than 100 million population resident outside Europe. A population that was subjugated by cannon, bayonet, and intrigue.*

"*Nor is Russia a democracy. Its one hundred ten million persons are dominated by a party of communists numbering less than two million. If the conscience of Americans is offended because the principles of real democracy, of self-determination, of home-rule, are being crushed to earth by the iron heel of German stormtroopers, let our indignation be impartial, and therefore virtuous. Let us lament over the plight of British, French, and Russian victims of conquest, who since the battle of Plassey in 1757, to the massacre of Moscow in 1923, have been appealing for liberty and justice and sympathy to the deafened ears of civilization.*

"'If the imperial conquest by Great Britain and France, and the diabolical persecution by Soviet Russia, are the outstanding examples of European democracy, then it is my opinion that the sooner that type of hypocrisy perishes from the face of the Earth, the better for all mankind.'"

McHenry resisted the urge to clap sarcastically when her performance concluded. "Who was that?"

"Father Charles Coughlin. Do you know of him? He was once a very popular media figure in America."

"Yes, I know of him, but I was not a fan of the man." McHenry didn't know whether he might disagree with the entire speech, but he had no intention of being re-educated to Nazi ideals. He reminded himself again that he was in enemy territory. Any potential moral correctness would have to wait until he was truly free. He always thought of Coughlin as a Nazi apologist anyway, and an anti-Semite.

"Do you have everything memorized?" he asked. It was a flanking maneuver.

"My memory is better than yours."

He wondered if Nazi science was involved, but she left it at that, returning to the subject of Coughlin.

"One thing about Father Coughlin is that he was censored," she said. "His radio show was shut down, and then the postal system stopped sending his magazine through the mail. This, under a government that claims to support freedom of speech."

"We were in difficult times," he answered. "Censorship is an unfortunate measure. The country had similar responses to the first world war. Those wartime restrictions were lifted after the emergency had passed. I have no doubt that the same thing will happen after this war."

"I'm glad to hear you say that," she replied coolly. "The rest of the world — and not just Germans — saw no sense in your First Amendment. Even other western nations took a more circumspect position on freedom of expression than some Americans did, realizing that often free speech must yield to other values and the need for order. Your own history suggests that they might have a point."

"Wait a second," he interrupted. "What do you mean, 'the rest of the world?' You've annexed every country!"

"That was over a process that took centuries," she countered. "Much of it was through diplomacy as various cultures became integrated, much like Germany's union with Austria in 1938. In your day, Hitler was more than willing to leave other peoples to their own determination."

"Like France and Poland?"

"Sam, those countries started this war. Poland took a portion of German territory after the first world war. It was German territory populated by German-speaking people. Hitler tried very hard to find a diplomatic solution."

McHenry stirred. Dale straightened up in her seat. Even without trying, she towered over him in their seats.

She was speaking quickly now. "It is the English and French imperialists that decided to go to war over Poland. And yet, after so many dead, Roosevelt and Churchill have secretly decided, if they won the war, they would give half of Poland to Stalin. England gave up its original rationale for fighting. As for France, it was they that declared war on Germany. And when they finally chose peace, Hitler gave them very generous terms."

"By occupying Paris," he interrupted.

"That was fully intended to be temporary. You're a military officer. You can see that Germany needed a buffer along the coast while the English were preparing an invasion. As it was, Hitler offered to turn Paris and the southern coasts back to unoccupied France. They were still negotiating that when the English and the Americans invaded France's unoccupied African colonies."

"You're talking about Operation Torch," McHenry noted skeptically. He knew of the invasion of North Africa. McHenry had not yet been in theater at that time, but his fellow Tuskegee airmen had played a role in its aftermath. Parker had sometimes spoken of it.

"Yes," she said smoothly. "Operation Torch. That was an illegal invasion."

"What?" McHenry laughed. "What do you mean, 'illegal'? We're at war."

"America was not at war with France. Unoccupied France was a neutral country in 1942. The French people wanted peace. They had taken themselves out of the war. Nevertheless, Roosevelt and Churchill wanted to attack the German Afrika Korps, but in getting there they chose to invade the French territories of Africa. Those were French soldiers they were fighting against, not Germans. *Neutral* French soldiers," she emphasized.

"Hardly neutral. Vichy France is a puppet government."

"Call it what you like now; the United States had formally recognized it as a neutral government. Those were unoccupied French territories that they invaded."

McHenry wasn't willing to be taken in. He reached for another bite while he might work on a good response. He didn't feel he needed one. He was never going to accept a moral equivalence between Nazi invasions and an American one. *Never*. He pondered this while it seemed she was waiting. But then — out of the blue — she startled him:

"It's not your fault, Sam. You'd been subjected to too much Jewish propaganda coming out of New York and Hollywood."

He put his fork down, fixing his eyes on hers, wondering how the conversation had taken this particular turn.

"This war would never have started if not for the Jews," she added emphatically.

"You're still blaming everything on Jews?" It was more of a statement than a question. "I thought you said racism was over. Didn't you say something like it being a thousand years?" he asked, mockingly.

"This isn't racism at all," she quickly insisted, apparently as startled as McHenry for having revealed this side of herself. "It's an observation of the facts of your times, not ours. The Jews are in control of most of your radio and newspapers, and virtually all of

Hollywood. Have you seen the number of anti-German movies they are making?"

McHenry rolled his eyes. "We're at war with the Germans. What kind of people would we be if Hollywood didn't make movies supporting the war effort? And how many of those movies did they make *before* the war started? I don't recall many." Then he remembered one, correcting himself. "Wait, I did see one, a James Stewart picture. They barely dared mention that it was in Germany. Heck of a conspiracy they have there. I can't believe the Reich was afraid of that."

"It's not so simple. This wasn't just the early Reich. Most Americans in your time are just as worried about the Jewish control of news and entertainment."

"They're not worried enough to stop watching those pictures and listening to those radio programs. And they're certainly not worried enough to lock up Jewish families and railroad them out of the country."

"It's definitely a different situation in America," Dale conceded. "But even now, in the middle of a war that you wish most Americans could continue to support, the majority of those Americans — sixty-five percent — agree that the Jews are at least partly to blame for Germany's restrictive policies."

"Sixty-five percent? How would you know that?" The number was no surprise to McHenry, but he was shocked that she would have any number at all. He was reminded of the device they used to display the image of the alien ship out of his memory. "Have you been scanning everybody's brains, too?"

She laughed, obviously trying to make the talk light again. "No. Your country has these quaint public opinion polls. We take that all in. And, quite frankly, we also access all radio, and most of the world's telephone systems. Rechners listen to nearly every conversation. They catalog the attitudes revealed in what people are talking about."

"Like I said, you've got an answer for everything." He took the remaining two bites of his steak and washed it down with soda.

"And like I was saying," she replied, "we certainly did make mistakes along the way. I won't argue with that. The invasion of Russia was almost a catastrophe. But there were reasons for that which were valid at that time. We do the best we can. That's all anybody can do. All I am saying is that you shouldn't judge Adolf Hitler, or us, by the lies that those American politicians — white politicians — put into your mind."

*

McHenry left the SS section unsure of whether he had accomplished anything with Dale. He had intended to impress upon her how important it was to rescue Parker. He hoped that she may help to avoid what had happened to that Italian. Now he wondered whether she was setting him up to forgive them if they allow Parker to die. *What was that bit about lies from white politicians anyway?* It had sounded so very hollow, coming from a white woman with a swastika on her sleeve.

He entered the zero-gravity hangar and saw Vinson and Bamberg waving to him from the hatch of the second Tiger. Their grins disappeared when they saw the glum expression on his face. No one spoke until he had spanned the distance.

"Did you have bad news?" asked Vinson.

"I'm not sure," McHenry answered. "She said they won't know for a while."

Bamberg motioned them inside. They took seats in the cockpit, and positioned them in a semi-circle, strapping themselves in place as was their custom. Another custom was to start with a cup of coffee. Vinson ordered those from memory while McHenry explained how his meeting went with Dale, with all the details intact.

"I don't mind the propaganda," McHenry concluded. "I just want to make sure they really care about Parker."

"I am sure she cares," said Vinson.

"She will not be making the final decision," said Bamberg. "I am sure she cares, too, but she will do her duty, whatever that is."

106

"We would all do our duty," Vinson maintained.

"And I am sure Herr McHenry would too," said Bamberg. He laughed and turned to McHenry. "You are our friend, and I am sure you will become a loyal citizen of the Reich once we return to our time. But I do not doubt you would escape *Göring* if the rechner ever gave you the opportunity."

McHenry smiled and nodded. "Maybe so, but all I'm asking is that the SS give their approval. Am I really being too suspicious?"

"She was probably telling the truth about the delay," replied Bamberg. "We recover satellites frequently. They sometimes order special recall missions before the scheduled retrieval dates. Current information is very important to them. That, however, does not mean the SS is being entirely candid."

"What do you mean," asked McHenry.

"Nothing improper, of course. The SS serves many functions. They maintain public order and they also run the Reich's intelligence service. They are the hands of the *Führer*."

"What about the SS troops who were fighting in the war?"

"That was a long time ago," said Bamberg. "For us, that is. There is a military branch called the Waffen-SS. They were very large during your war but, over the centuries, most of its operations became obsolete. We no longer have a *Heer* or *Kriegsmarine* at all, which you would call an army and navy. Land and sea warfare have become almost obsolete. The Waffen-SS itself is now used solely for special operations of the SS."

"They have a few small starships," added Vinson.

"Yes," said Bamberg. "There are rumors that they have been running surveys on the Far Wall, but that is the extent of the Waffen-SS. Have you heard of the Far Wall?"

"Vinson told me about a wall in space that no ship can pass through and return from," said McHenry, nodding to Vinson. "Why the Waffen-SS, and not the Luftwaffe?"

"It gives them something to do," laughed Bamberg, momentarily turning his eyes to a visible portion of the entryway. "It is always ideology with those people. In any case, the SS is big, and it is involved in everything. I understand that *Oberführer* Mtubo had been a Waffen-SS officer until he was assigned to this project. He might even have been working on the Far Wall but I do not know that for sure. We only know from rumors when the mission began. Most of these here are with the intelligence branch. They would be using an SS ship for this mission if they had one large enough."

"Are there any Gestapo on this ship?"

"Not that I am aware of. That is part of a completely different branch of the SS."

"You might see them occasionally when we are back home," said Vinson. "But most SS that you will see are with the police."

That evoked a thought in McHenry. "Do you think there might be some people — humans, I mean — who support the Grauen?"

"It is possible," said Bamberg. "But I hope never to meet one who does."

Vinson and Bamberg had exchanged grim glances and those expressions became fixed into McHenry's mind. Clearly, treason was something no one could countenance. He thought about how Bamberg had so easily brushed off the possibility that he might still want to escape, even though they had become good friends. Duty was so deeply ingrained into these men. He wondered whether that was in their genes, deliberately so, and concluded almost instantly that it probably was.

He now regretted having steered the conversation in this direction, as he needed to return to his point.

"So, can I trust the SS?"

Bamberg nodded. "You can trust them to operate in the best interest of the *Führer*."

"I see," said McHenry, even though he didn't. He knew only that the answer would really depend upon the interests of the *Führer*. Perhaps that was the best answer he could have gotten. *Would the Führer care?* he wondered. He couldn't see why.

"I think I see, too," said Bamberg. "You believe there is some ulterior motive to the collecting of people from the past."

"The thought occurred to me."

"Then put that out of your mind. We are going to be on this mission, on this ship, for at least five years. You are a pleasant diversion for the crew. Our entertainment."

"But what about Dale trying to indoctrinate me?"

"Probably because she likes it. She is in the SS. They like to be ideological. It's their nature." Bamberg turned momentarily to Vinson, "Sorry. It's true."

"It is part of her charm," Vinson shrugged.

McHenry sat back, considering how to broach the subject, and then decided to simply say what he thought. "You can't tell me there is no propaganda value for when you return to your millennium. The Reich can parade us all around like trophy pieces."

Bamberg laughed. "Such as might have been in your time. There is little need for that in the future. I can assure you, when the folk want to see such trophies, the rechners can present them in any form. They can create — what you think of as movies — of people saying anything they want them to say. It is like the simulator here except with images of people. You would not know the difference."

"You mean," McHenry began, "they could change the ending to *Casablanca* to where the Germans win?"

"Yes, they can, although it sounds like one they would have simply erased. They can do that even in your time."

*

CHAPTER 15

"When the moon is full it throws its swath of gold across the lovely Mediterranean, and sometimes the nights are so calm and moontinged and gentle that you cannot remember or believe that the purpose of everything around you is death."
— *Ernie Pyle, war correspondent, (April 19, 1944)*

Wednesday, April 19, 1944

McHenry met Dale for breakfast the next day. He was upbeat, having decided that the *Führer* probably had more things to worry about than Parker. If true, the decision would be put squarely into the realm of science. That could still be a problem, he thought, but Parker would get a fair chance by the SS. His friends in the Luftwaffe would then do their very best to save his life.

The sad expression on Dale's face gave him the news before she could even say the words. "I'm so sorry, Sam."

He sat at the table and slumped. Any pretense of defiance as a P.O.W. had disappeared from his mind days ago. Now he was giving up the pride he had felt as a man who had risen to the most unusual of situations. He had so much looked forward to sharing this experience with Parker, showing him the future, the Earth from 22,000 miles above, and then teaching him to fly through space.

She held her long fingers over his hand. "Let's talk over lunch."

"I'm not hungry."

"You still need to eat," she said warmly. She then instructed the machine to give them both the same meals they had the last time they breakfasted together.

"I didn't know you could do that," he said.

"It remembers everything."

He didn't eat right away, but he did take a sip from his soda. The cold drink was refreshing. He never guessed the effect was designed

110

to subtly ease the stress on his nervous system. In that respect, the meal was not entirely the same one he had the day before.

"I was looking forward to showing him the wonders you have. He would have loved the food."

"Do you really believe he would have liked being here?" she asked gently.

"It's better than dying," he said.

"I don't think you felt that way at first. He may never." She looked for any response and then continued. "The things that are important to you might not be important to him."

"He's still better off here than dying in the water."

"I'm sorry, Sam. I wish we could have done it. All of us do. But we also have to think about the security of the Reich."

"I don't expect anyone to take risks for me or my friend. All I wanted was a fair shake."

"We did that," she insisted. "We tried everything. I'm just so sorry that we couldn't find a way."

McHenry heard the desperation in her voice and believed her. "No," he said. "I should apologize. I knew this could happen. I should really thank you for trying. Everyone. Please tell all the SS people that I thank them, too."

She seemed pleased, or at least relieved, at his thoughtful words. "Sam," she said after a pause, "We of the SS are calling the regiment to parade. It's a function to celebrate Adolf Hitler's birthday. The main watch room will be converted into a temporary review field. A few of the senior Luftwaffe staff will be there, too. I know that you may not appreciate our first *Führer* the way that we do but I do think you should attend. You might enjoy it."

He wasn't in the mood to celebrate Hitler's birthday but he nodded his head. "Yes, I'll be there," he said.

"Good! It's a formal military event. You'll do me the courtesy of standing at attention when we're in formation, won't you?"

"I always stand for the *Kommandant*," he noted. "You've seen it yourself whenever somebody around here shouts '*Achtung!*' The Geneva Convention demands prisoners respect proper military formality. Heck, I even get up when everyone else is standing for those ridiculous morning *Führer* speeches — including by Hitler himself — and you know I hate that. I'm not going to Heil Hitler but I won't embarrass you either."

She smiled tenderly, then looked down at his garment. "Rechner, Herr McHenry will need special attire for the *Führertag* event. Give him a dark blue civilian suit when he gets ready for it. And give it some yellow trim." She looked back into his eyes and smiled. "You'll look good in that. It's very stylish in our time."

"When is Hitler's birthday?"

"Oh Sam!" she said, raising her voice just a bit. "That's the first thing we should have taught you. It's the twentieth of April. That's tomorrow."

*

Barr swung the Tiger gently to the east, heading to the last satellite on the recall list.

"Fifty seconds," he reported to Mallory, the SS man beside him. At their present velocity, relative to orbit, they could have every satellite on the recall list inside the ship in record time. Anxious to complete the mission, Barr already had his finger on the satellite trap control.

This probe was a small one, an SB-27. Like all satellites on this mission, it was black as night, wrapped in an unterkarbon net, and virtually undetectable. Even active sensors would require a distance of less than fifty meters. They would have to rely almost entirely on the position recorded in the manifest and hope it hadn't drifted too far. Barr set the trap to snag the probe. They were closing in. He tweaked the stick one more time and programmed a final breaking maneuver.

The field wake alarm startled them. Far below them, a Grauen ship was lighting up its interstellar drive while leaving Earth's atmosphere. Barr released the throttle and the shuttle coasted. Maybe they wouldn't be seen. Mallory targeted the main guns dead center on the enemy ship, just in case.

Rules of engagement were complicated. If they destroyed a Grauen ship here, one thousand years in their past, history would be changed. But simply being noticed by a Grauen ship could do that as well. The SS man would make the decision whether to fire.

"He doesn't see us," said Mallory, watching the blip on the dome.

"*Ja.*" Barr agreed. It seemed like the Grauen would leave them alone. No one really knew the limits of Grauen technology. Weren't they millions of years ahead of the Reich? But then how could they not be aware of the Tiger's presence? If they were, they didn't act like it. Or maybe they just didn't want to fight. It looked to Barr as though Mallory certainly didn't. He decided to just let the Tiger coast until the Grauen ship was long gone.

They would miss the satellite but that was okay. A firefight with a Grauen here had to be avoided at all costs.

It might take almost an hour for Barr to return to position. This would normally be a fifteen-second maneuver but time was no longer the priority. He carefully plotted a course that would veer away from their original direction, all the while minimizing the energy use that might expose their position.

It would require another orbit. Maybe two. For Barr, the only good thing about the trip was that the SS man beside him kept quiet for now.

*

"You would have enjoyed meeting him," McHenry told Vinson. They sat alone in the Tiger discussing his disappointment.

"In some ways, I feel that I did meet him," said Vinson. "He was the one who followed you down into the water, wasn't he? I was listening from below."

"He's the one."

"I remember listening to his steady voice. He personally called that ship they sent after you. I am sure they worked faster because of his presence. Kathy — I mean *Sturmbannführer* Dale — was laughing

113

because he ranked lower than the ship's captain. But he never identified his rank, and they were so very deferential to him."

That provoked McHenry to smile. "They probably thought he was white." It had happened before, he remembered. Almost all military officers were white, so it's easy to make that assumption. Even a Tuskegee airman could fall victim to it.

"You never talk about your experience living under racism," Vinson observed.

"What is there to talk about? It's lousy." It was not so much that McHenry didn't want to discuss it. As much as he liked Vinson, he didn't want to degrade his own country to a man who was, in effect, a soldier of a country the United States was at war with.

"Well, then," Vinson said, eager to get back to the subject of flying. "We will set up for another descent exercise. Even with unterkarbon around you, you will need a lot more practice before you can evade the Grauen."

*

"Two minutes," Barr reported.

"*Ja,*" was the simple reply.

He looked over at Mallory, saw him studying the manifest, and then turned his attention to the satellite.

They would be coming in slowly this time. It was a risk to return to the same area as before, but a necessary one. The Grauen's field wake had come too close to the satellite. It certainly would have drifted. The longer they wait, the further it might stray. But how far had it gone? The machine would plot the best guess but there was no way to expect accuracy out of these measurements. A field wake was not a phenomenon of normal space, and therefore its influence could not be in the realm of normal physics.

"Sixty seconds." Barr applied more braking and extended the trap. They were practically crawling now. He switched the display mode to a tactical view and the dome washed out the continents on the Earth below. The flight path projected on the dome began to split. The rechner could no longer compute the expected position as one straight line.

"Why so slow?" asked Mallory.

"That Grauen field wake jarred the satellite's orbit," Barr explained. "We cannot have a fix unless we get really close. We may have to make several passes or wait for it to realign."

"Why are you only finding out now?"

Barr took a deep breath. "We knew there would be a deviation when the Grauen passed us."

"I did not know that."

"Well, why did you think we were coming in so slowly?"

Mallory didn't have time for an answer, even if he had one. An alarm sounded again, only this time it was a damage alarm. They had just hit the satellite.

"*Scheiss!*" shouted Barr. But it was worse than that. The satellite's unterkarbon net tore loose from its mount and a few of its fibers touched inside the Tiger's open cargo hold. Barr's status display lit up in a way he had only seen in a simulation. The unterkarbon was reacting to the normal matter. He jettisoned the cargo, a rack of satellites they'd taken in before. But it wasn't enough.

"What do I do?" asked Mallory.

"Just man the guns," Barr said angrily. Seconds ticked by and the display indicated more trouble was brewing. The Tiger's engines were affected, which Barr took to mean a failure of the power system. Or was it? Three percent of the engines were out. Then four percent, and then five. *What was going on?*

Like most modern systems, the unterkarbon was linked using nanotechnology structures — tiny machines created at the molecular level. These satellites were programmed to self-destruct in the event of an emergency. *Did that programming extend to fragments in the net?* Barr couldn't know, but it made sense and it was all he had to go on.

"Hold on!" he shouted. Without waiting for an okay from Mallory, he powered up the engines near the affected area. They were pushed against the left sides of their seats. This was unusual. These engines were designed to provide propulsion without a reaction. It was never supposed to feel like they were moving.

"What's happening?" asked Mallory — more shouting than asking.

Gee forces pushed hard but Barr spoke calmly. "I am running the engines out of phase. I believe the unterkarbon contaminants have reached the engines aft of the cargo hold. I am trying to overload that section."

"What good would that do? That is only a chemical reaction. You need a nuclear one to destroy the unterkarbon."

"I am not trying to destroy it," Barr said, still able to maintain his calm even though they were now tumbling wildly fast. "It is creating a slow reaction on its own. I only want to fuse the nano units so they stop working against me." He had been watching the engine power systems. Failures had risen to eight percent but they stopped climbing for long enough to be sure that the danger had passed. Barr shut down the engines again.

"We should have self-destructed," said Mallory, recovering from his dizziness. "You emitted too much energy with that maneuver of yours. We could have been detected."

"Our people need to be told about that Grauen. When I die for the Reich, it will not be for a stupid reason."

"Don't you think they've seen it, too?"

"We are on the other side of the planet," said Barr angrily. "And they need to see these field wake numbers." That was technically correct, he realized, but it was a convenient excuse nevertheless. He thought about McHenry, the bird that almost killed him in that old airplane, and the enormous odds against that happening. If a man had to meet death on a mission, it should be while fighting and not as the victim of a freak accident.

He took a moment to make plans to retrieve the satellites he had ejected. They were going to be very late getting back.

*

116

McHenry and Vinson left the Tiger after an hour, pausing at the hatch. The hangar was empty. One of the Tigers was still missing but the second one was shut down.

"There should be someone here," said Vinson. "A second Tiger is supposed to be ready to launch."

"Something must have gone wrong," suggested McHenry.

"Let's go see where everybody is." Vinson made his way along the handholds on the railing and called to the rechner. He asked it a question in German while McHenry worked furiously to keep up with his fast movements.

They found Sanchez at a second hatch, still in the null-gravity section of the ship. McHenry had never been in this section before, although it wasn't far from the hangar area. Some of the exterior hatches could be accessed here. Sanchez was looking at a display panel on the wall.

"The unterkarbon will not retract," she explained. "It was damaged and they had to dock outside"

"Damaged? How?"

"That is the interesting part." She looked to McHenry. "They saw your Geier. It did not see them but its field wake moved the satellite. The Tiger ran into it."

"And that damaged the Tiger?" asked McHenry.

"Unterkarbon nets are fragile at certain points," said Sanchez. "Not as fragile as your P-40 but it is fairly sensitive. It is possible, although still unlikely, that they know we are here."

Vinson put his hand on a panel, activating a screen on the wall. "Why are we still in condition three? We should be preparing to leave orbit."

Sanchez snickered. "Maybe you should tell that to the *Kommandant*."

"Who was piloting?" asked McHenry.

"It was Barr," said Sanchez. "He is in debrief with the SS."

"About a mechanical problem?" he asked.

"From the mouths of babes," she laughed.

The men and women of the inspection team eventually came through the second outside hatch, still wearing space suits. McHenry recognized them, once they'd opened their helmets, having spoken with them before.

"The unterkarbon contaminated the drive system," one reported to Sanchez, but speaking in English for McHenry's benefit.

"The entire underside was ripped but still functional," said a woman beside him. "We just did a repair to strengthen it."

"Is the passage secure?" asked Sanchez. "Can we go in?"

"Yes, everything is clear," replied the first man. "There is already somebody in there now."

"The passage is locked to Lieutenant McHenry," warned a harsh voice. It was the rechner.

"*Jawohl!*" Sanchez replied. She turned to McHenry, smiling. "See? The rechner understands you are already a good enough pilot to steal a Tiger."

The others laughed, as did McHenry. He felt some pride, but he also felt sad. It was another reminder that escape was impossible. The rechner would make certain of that.

"Not to worry," said the space-suited woman. "We might be doing an overhaul. The rechner will probably let you in while the Tiger is down for maintenance."

The hatch opened just as they were about to leave. It was an SS officer carrying a tablet. He nodded in acknowledgment to them as he rushed through past them. There was something on his face that McHenry hadn't seen since his arrival. He didn't show the confidence that the others always had.

It almost looked like fear.

*

CHAPTER 16

NAZIS AND HOLY PLACES

Once more the President has spelled out American policy regarding the bombing of Rome. It is unfortunate that this explanation must be repeated again and again, but enemy propaganda makes that necessary....

The current Gallup Poll of American public opinion — covering Protestants, Catholics and non-church members — shows that only 19 per cent disapprove the bombing of European religious places when it is considered necessary by our military leaders. That minority should study prayerfully the President's statement.

— *The Pittsburgh Press, (April 20, 1944)*

Thursday, April 20, 1944

McHenry returned to his room and dropped himself into his chair. It was after midnight, but he didn't feel tired at all. He stared out at the Earth and studied the weather patterns. He desperately wanted to forget Parker. It would have been bad enough if Parker had been killed unexpectedly, but McHenry already knew the place and the time.

"Rechner, what can you tell me about the men that the SS wants to bring back?"

"Information on fifteen men on the retrieval schedule is available from public historical sources."

He heard the words and remembered that the machine sometimes takes things literally. "I meant men and women."

"Information on twenty-five men and women on the retrieval schedule is available from public historical sources."

"Thank you," he said, determined to be more careful. "Can you give it to me on a *Klemmbrett?*"

McHenry grabbed the tablet that had appeared from the slot and started reading. It was separated into sections, each of which was about a specific person. It was very thorough: Family trees, newspaper articles and personnel records. Some included photos, and some did not. All of it had been translated into English for him. The machine never forgot that he didn't speak German, although he believed he was picking it up.

He found his own records in the mix, all neatly typed. It was more thorough than he expected, although he initially thought the Purple Heart listed in his awards was an error. He saw two lists of the faculty from his grade school, with names of teachers he had forgotten about and others he remembered fondly. His military service records were all there, including his medical record and flight logs. The last entry showed his presumed death on that doomed flight. It was recorded as a mechanical error due to battle damage. *That explains the Purple Heart,* he thought. He wasn't certain he was due the medal, but gathered that Parker had pushed for it.

"Rechner," he called presently. "How about a cup of hot chocolate?"

He would often end his day with a luxurious cup of hot chocolate in his room, sipping while staring out into space and contemplating on the events of the day. Rather than dive back into the material on the tablet, McHenry thought for a moment about the machine. It had fascinated him more than once, but he had never taken the time to study the technology itself or the limitations on its use.

The machine controlled all the equipment aboard *Göring.* Everything: The slots that provided food and drinks, the screens on the walls, elevators, even the lights, and probably the propulsion and control of the ship itself. The machine had more than just intelligence. It also held responsibility.

This much seemed obvious now. What didn't seem so obvious before was that the machine was always making decisions before carrying out those functions, and taking in his reactions. It was only a matter of time before McHenry would connect the dots. He now realized that he couldn't trust the machine the way he did before.

He didn't know whether it would ever lie to him, although he suspected that it could. He was sure, however, that it would tell him only as much as it wanted him to know. He began reading the materials again from the beginning. Only this time he would look for whatever was missing.

But a lot was missing. Not every name included school records, and even his own school records were incomplete. This made sense to him, as most of this information would have been discarded over the years. Then he went to his military records. They did appear to be complete. That also made sense. After all, the Army never throws anything away. McHenry decided to put all his efforts there and prepared for a long read.

It was a long read, and it seemed like a pointless exercise. Then he scanned the tablet for other Americans in the list. There were three others, but only two in the military, and their files were also long and boring. One was a Navy pilot, lost in the Pacific theater, and the other was a soldier who lost his leg and then died on the sea voyage home after the war ended.

"Rechner, can a man who lost his leg get a new one?"

"Yes," it answered. "The medical facilities aboard *Göring* are equipped to replace limbs."

Well, he thought, at least that's one man who would definitely appreciate the trip. Then he considered what Dale had said about Parker. He might not want to be rescued. Of course she was right. Parker was a devout Christian. He expects to wake up in Heaven and meet Jesus Christ, not that black Nazi Mtubo. McHenry was set to ponder the morality of letting Parker die just to let him avoid this mean spectacle, but he just realized what was missing in those records. There had been no mention of religion anywhere.

He scanned back, remembering the words that were printed on the first page of his real personnel records. Even his dog tags had a single-letter abbreviation for religion. It was on everyone's file. It had to be readily accessible just in case a chaplain was called. But they weren't listed here. It was a curious omission. Why did the friend of that Italian's die? Would they allow Parker to die because he was a devout man? It was a cruel thought.

The soldiers' and the pilots' records didn't list a religion either. He read every line just to be sure, but he was already sure. He then went back through the military records of the Germans, and the Italians and the Japanese. No religions were listed anywhere.

"Rechner!" he said sternly, tucking the *Klemmbret* under his arm. "I'm going to see *Sturmbannführer* Dale. You might want to warn her that I'm on my way." Being already mad, he put an emphasis on the word *Sturmbannführer*. He was going to be madder if what he suspected to be true turned out to be true in fact. Pronouncing the name of that Nazi rank just put a steam iron onto his mood.

*

Dale was waiting for him at the SS officers' mess. It was a good thing, he realized. He might have had trouble finding her elsewhere.

"Is something wrong?" she asked. He gathered that she already knew that. She had remained standing, which was not usually the case.

"Did the machine tell you I was in a foul mood?"

"Yes," she said, looking at the tablet in his hand. "Rechner, two cups of coffee."

"No thanks," said McHenry, but the cups were already on their way out.

She took a seat and slid one cup toward him. "Oh, you'd better. We might as well talk for a while. It might help you think better, and I need a break myself."

"I have a problem," he said, taking a seat. He moved his cup closer just to be cordial. "I was looking at this list of people you're bringing back. You people seem to have everything. Funny thing is, this list doesn't include any religious information."

"It's a summary. The list doesn't have their bowling scores either," she said.

"Not exactly true. I've seen sports scores in the newspaper articles."

"Only because it was in the article," she replied. "But, look, I don't know why the rechner puts some things in there and leaves other things out. Rechners do things by their own logic. It may be that it considered this subject a personal matter. Or perhaps it doesn't want to prejudice you. It knows you're going to be meeting these people."

"So, you're telling me that some of these people are religious?"

"No, Sam," she sighed. "I just don't want you to get the impression that this is that important a consideration for us. So many men died in that foul war that we can pick and choose from the ones we think would assimilate well. But it's only a minor consideration. If you seriously believe we wouldn't recover your friend because of this..."

"That's exactly what I believe," he said firmly.

"You're wrong, Sam," she insisted. "It's just not important in that way. Did the Army tell you we had laws against religion? There are many religious people in the Reich. Why would we care?"

McHenry was no longer steaming, but he still didn't trust her. "Okay. How many religious people do you have on this ship?"

She paused, taking another sip from her coffee and then glancing at his untouched coffee cup. "None, but that's different. They're not in the Luftwaffe or the SS. But something you need to understand is that people started giving up those customs and superstitions when they started living longer. It became emotionally unnecessary once humanity gained immortality — and that was a long time ago.

"I told you that your friend wouldn't like it here," she continued. "But that was just an honest assessment. His religion wasn't a problem for us. Or, frankly, it wasn't a deciding issue. We would have given him the counseling he needed. The American army must have told you more lies about national socialism, Sam. It just isn't the way that you think."

McHenry couldn't accept that. Some of it did make sense, but the question of the missing religious information still didn't ring true.

"Even for the Jews?" he asked, still wary.

"Your friend wasn't a Jew."

"I know that," he said. "I'm just asking. Did the Army lie about that?"

"You'd better have some of your coffee," she said. "You might be up for a while, and I know that you need sleep."

He did as she suggested and then motioned her to continue.

"Sam, as I've conceded, Hitler didn't like the Jews. It was a deep-seated prejudice, the kind that was common in the twentieth-century. You've experienced something like it yourself, and you know that the Jews aren't well liked in America either. It was only worse in Europe. The problem is that they didn't like Hitler either. They weren't legally citizens, and those who stayed in Germany became a security risk. One Jew assassinated a German diplomat and that set off anger in the streets. They needed to be placed into camps for the Reich's security as well as their own protection."

"What did they *do* to them?" McHenry insisted.

"The war wasn't going too well for us at this point," she explained. "You know this. You were a part of it. We were fighting a multi-front war. You made it very hard to get supplies."

"And now it's our fault?"

"Well, frankly, yes," she replied. "Even before the war, America would take in very few Jews. The resettlement camps became overcrowded. Disease took its toll. Many died of disease, typhus mostly."

"How many?"

"Altogether? Probably a million. No one knows the exact number."

He took another sip of coffee but said nothing. It was hard to comprehend. He had never dealt with numbers in the millions until he started learning to fly the Luftwaffe's Tigers. Those were energy quantities and distance measurements, not men, women and children.

"Yes, you do know the number," he said suddenly. "You're cataloging individuals. Your machines watch everything. You said so yourself. You said you had the next two years mapped out."

"Sam, keep in mind that this war will kill tens of millions. Many will die in combat, many will die in the cities that are bombed, and many will starve for lack of food. Half a million Germans starved after the first world war because the English and French blocked relief supplies — and that was *after* that war was already over. Wars are terrible things."

She continued, cutting off any reply. "Do not forget that the English were excellent agitators. The Russians, too. Wars require the support of the people, and for that they create propaganda. They planted many false stories. This is common. I'm sure the Germans did it, too."

McHenry studied her face. She seemed uneasy about this. It was no doubt a difficult subject for her, but he wondered how much of that unease was more from the difficulty in explaining this away. He also assumed that Nazi historians had very likely sanitized the number dead. The number was likely closer to the millions he had heard before. He also understood something else.

"I don't believe it," he said.

"War does terrible things," she repeated.

"That's not what I mean," he corrected. "You've often noticed how I'm not yet at home here in your future. Things that are normal for you are surprises for me. I knew that you were really old but I was still shocked when you told me you had grandchildren. You look so young."

Her head tilted, as though marked by curiosity.

"See?" he said, examining her expression. "In my time, older women would be pleased when someone notices that they look young. Or at least they would react differently. Okay, so looking young isn't so special here. It's a lot like that with your physics. Where I come from, this ship is impossible. Traveling faster than light, or back in time, are thought impossible in my day. The very gravity on this ship is impossible. I'm not even sure what's more impossible, the gravity right here on this deck, or the way it ends sharply at the hangar. This is all going to take me a long time to get used to. But you aren't at home in my time either. You may be a historian, but you don't have the instincts of a person in the twentieth-century. Before the war, I'd been hit every day by advertisements in newspapers selling soap and cereal. I'm no easy mark. So let me tell you something: Millions of people cannot just die that way in Europe.

"No," he stopped himself immediately. "It actually takes more than starvation and disease. You may not realize this — your machines give you all the food you want — but most people in my time are able to take care of themselves if they're allowed to. Poor people in my country live in shacks with dirt floors but they don't die by the millions. Those Jews were moved out of their positions in a modern society to a place where they could not provide for themselves. If you could not take care of them then you should have let them go. To allow that many to die is unconscionable."

"Nobody would take them, Sam. They tried. America wouldn't take them. But I do understand. I even told you we made mistakes. This was a difficult war. The history of America isn't perfect either. Even now, your country is holding thousands of American families in camps simply because their ancestors were from Japan. They're holding still more from Germany and Italy who tried to become citizens."

"How many are dying from typhus?"

"Different set of economics," she replied. "Then you have to consider the earlier sins of America's past: Slavery, wars, the confiscation of Indian lands."

"That was many years ago."

"Sam," she sighed. "To us, all those Jews died a thousand years ago. It's ancient history."

He took another sip from his coffee. "Can you really pass it off that easily?"

"It's a part of our history that had to be done."

"Had to be done? Do Jews think so too?" He stammered for a moment, suddenly pondering a horrendous thought. "Are there any left?"

Dale set her coffee cup down. "Rechner, please contact *Standartenführer* Stern. Request a meeting." She then turned to

126

McHenry, "One of his parents, a Canadian I believe, has Jewish blood."

A chime sounded. McHenry had learned that high-ranking officers had distinct tones to announce their presence.

"Herr *Standartenführer*," said Dale. "Herr McHenry is uncomfortable with the unfortunate events of the Hitler times, particularly with respect to the Jewish question. Would you be able to speak with him about this?"

"I see," answered Stern. "I will be happy to see him. Send him to my office."

"The 'Jewish question'?" prompted McHenry.

"Don't be so naive, Sam. Even in your day, that phrase had been around for hundreds of years. Henry Ford wrote a book about it. You should have read it."

Dale led him out the door, leaving their coffee cups on the table.

"Is this really necessary?" asked McHenry. He didn't think Stern would be any more forthcoming than she was.

"Yes," she replied. "This is a big deal to you. I don't want to leave any questions in your mind. It would be best if you get over this ancient history and move on with your new life."

*

Stern's private office was just off the main watch room. McHenry saw two large screens when they entered, but they quickly disappeared, dissolving as though they never existed.

"It is good to see you again Herr McHenry," said Stern.

"Likewise," McHenry replied perfunctorily.

Dale asked to be excused, adding the inevitable *Heil Renard!* McHenry caught a glimpse of the mysterious Mtubo beckoning to her in the hallway just as the door was closing behind her. Then he was left alone with Stern, having the impression this meeting might even have been planned somehow.

Stern took a seat and simultaneously motioned McHenry to do the same. "I understand you still feel some antagonism for our first *Führer.*"

"What I don't understand is, how could you not?" responded McHenry. It was more of a statement than a question.

"Why do you say that? Because one of my grandparents was a Jew? It is true that I am very fortunate. I do feel bad in that the progeny of those millions who died might otherwise have been as fortunate as me. Adolf Hitler performed a service for me and for all of the Jews who survived those times. You see, the hatred of the Jews did not begin with Adolf Hitler. That goes back thousands of years. This hatred forced the Jews to bind together, supporting one another, apart from the greater society in which they lived.

"They had a fable, perhaps you know of it, where a man named Abraham was ordered by their deity to kill his own son. The man was actually about to do it, hesitating just long enough for the deity to stop him. It was a test of loyalty, you see, but it was loyalty to a myth! Such fruitless loyalty stayed with the Jews for millennia, and what did it gain them? Only more hatred from the very real people who were not myths.

"You have seen them," he continued. "Wearing those little hats; praying in their temples to an imaginary deity; spending their entire lives in endless rituals that serve no purpose, and separating themselves from the greater society. Do you think I would want to live in such a group? I do not simply refuse to hate Adolf Hitler. On the contrary, I *thank* Adolf Hitler! Without him and his movement, I might be living in those dark ages."

"But millions of people!" McHenry exclaimed.

"Matters not!" Stern asserted. "Those are millions who might otherwise have been left to suffer a miserable existence. The greater society comes first; before groups, and before individuals. The Reich needed to survive. Say what you will but difficult decisions had to be made."

"You're seeming to admit that the number was in the millions, and that these deaths were deliberate."

"Yes." Stern smiled again. "You are quite right. You'll have to excuse *Sturmbannführer* Dale for not being candid with you. Due to her work, she knows more than she is permitted to disclose. She doesn't have the discretion that I do."

"In what way is this a military secret? If it was one thousand years ago to you, then why the censorship now?"

"What you think of as censorship is a way for the Reich to maintain order, unity and civility. It has always been that way, not only in our society, but in the world in general."

"Then why keep the exact number a secret?"

"This is not like a military secret. We simply choose not to dwell on it." Stern seemed to think for a few seconds, looking into the air above McHenry momentarily. "Just suppose the number was really ten million," he said after a pause. "Would you then say Hitler was ten times as bad as he would be if we only killed one million?

"And then what if the number was only half a million," he continued. "Would you then say that was half as bad as one million? You see, these numbers are of such a scale that the moral consequences cannot be judged on the basis of quantities. We dismiss the numbers and think only in terms of right and wrong. And for that you must judge the times. You do not possess the historical insight in which to judge the moral correctness of a man like Adolf Hitler."

"I don't need historical insight to say that such mass killing is wrong," said McHenry.

"Oh really?" Stern asked with a sneer. "If you like, I can have the rechner list the names of men you have killed for the American army. I can even give you the names of their families, widows, and orphans."

"That's not the same thing," McHenry insisted, startled but undeterred.

Stern leaned forward. "If you do not want to take my opinion on this matter, perhaps you should wait until we retrieve a couple of the Jews on our recovery schedule. You can argue with them about it."

"I was under the impression that you weren't picking up any religious people," said McHenry.

"We are not. The two Jews we plan to retrieve are both atheists."

"Why am I not surprised?" McHenry said sourly.

"It should prove interesting," said Stern. "They are also communists. They will not appreciate the Reich's victory any more than you do — not right away — but they will turn around just as you will when you learn more about the Reich."

"If you think so, then why not think the same of my friend Parker?"

"Is that what this is about?" Stern seemed surprised at that. "I assure you Herr McHenry. There are technical reasons why we cannot recover your friend. It has nothing whatsoever to do with his beliefs. You have my word on that."

McHenry didn't know what to say to that. He looked at the man, full of arrogance and confidence, and yet there was a touch of regret in his voice. That seemed to be the one thing he had said that sounded genuinely contrite.

"Believe me, we have no doubt that he could have become a loyal subject of the Reich, and perhaps one day, loyal to the *Führer*. You will learn to support our *Führer*, too. Everything she does is for us as a people. You will see. And the day will come when you will appreciate Adolf Hitler as well."

McHenry simply refused to believe that. "For a people who say you don't worship God, you sure seem to treat Hitler like one."

"Yes," answered Stern. He smiled contently and confidently. "I would gladly sacrifice the lives of my sons for Adolf Hitler. And without question, all my sons would do the same. But unlike the fabled Abraham, we would not hesitate long enough for our first *Führer* to change his mind."

*

Dale was present with Mtubo in the *Kommandant's* office when the Luftwaffe technical sergeant gave his report. *Kommandant Oberst* Volker stood beside Mtubo listening to the presentation. The rechner projected a diagram upon the *Kommandant's* desk. They were schematics for the Tiger engines, infected from the molecular corrosion.

"The damage is most extensive," the sergeant concluded. "But the unterkarbon net is the dilemma. We cannot repair the Tiger inside the hangar without retracting the unterkarbon, and we cannot retract the unterkarbon because the terminating matter is fused. Under present conditions, it will take at least twenty days to make repairs outside."

"May I ask a question, *Oberst*?" asked Dale. The SS aboard *Göring* rarely addressed Volker as *Kommandant*, at least not directly. Her rank was *Oberst*. She may have been the ship's commander, but she was not her commander. Dale continued after she nodded. "Can the unterkarbon be ejected at the hangar entrance?"

"It would expose us to the Grauen regardless," explained the *Kommandant*. "The net was designed to retract precisely at the hangar doors. The geometry is critical, and the tolerances are tight. This is not just with respect to shape, but the Tiger's center of gravity as well. A variation of five millimeters could render us detectable within two thousand kilometers, and that is by our understanding of the Grauen sensors. Those intelligence estimates could always be wrong."

"I understand that, *Oberst*," she said respectfully. "But the temporary measures are also risky. We have just heard that *Göring's* unterkarbon envelope has been compromised by the placement of the Tiger docked beside it. That may only be a difference of a half-kilometer but this is an additional half-kilometer over a period of weeks, rather than just the few minutes of greater exposure while the unterkarbon is withdrawn." She glanced at Mtubo, who seemed to nod approval at her making the point.

The *Kommandant* took a brief pause before responding, clearly surprised by Dale's grasp of the details. "Yes," she said. "That is a valid concern. It is always on my mind. There is, however, another problem as this geostationary orbit represents an additional security risk. If they are looking for us at all, they will be looking at this altitude first. My orders for this mission are risk-averse to the extreme. This ship, and its mission, may ultimately be the last defense of the Reich. I cannot allow us to break cover for even an instant. Not here."

"I understand," she answered. "I withdraw my point."

"It would be much more secure if we pulled back to deep space," the *Kommandant* noted. "Take it somewhere that we may tear off the unterkarbon, bring the Tiger inside, and then be back here within a day. Working through the airlock could take months."

Mtubo looked to Dale, who shook her head. "I would not advise leaving until the events of June."

"Understood," said the *Kommandant*. "Alternatively, we can also jettison the Tiger into the sun." She saw Mtubo's eyes shift briefly to the technical sergeant and then back again. The *Kommandant* took the point and turned to the sergeant. "Thank you *Feldwebel*. Continue the repairs outside. Dismissed."

Mtubo spoke after the sergeant had left the office. "Operation Spartacus would require at least two Tigers. It is too soon to lose one now."

"Is there any change in that mission contingency?"

"There might indeed be," Mtubo sighed. He turned to Dale. "*Sturmbannführer*, you are dismissed."

"*Heil Renard!*" said Dale, clicking her heels before turning and leaving the room. She knew what the topic of discussion would be, and she was glad she didn't have to be present for it.

She had a feeling they might be leaving in June after all.

*

Too disturbed to even think about sleeping, McHenry left the SS section and went up to the hangar section. He needed a friend to talk to. The zero-gee hangar section was deserted except for an Asian Luftwaffe officer aboard one of the Tigers who told him a few of the pilots went to the crippled Tiger.

One of the outer hatches opened for him. Could the rechner have made a mistake? McHenry floated through and then followed a makeshift gangway that curved slightly into the familiar hatch of the

Tiger. He paused there, looking at the opening. It was just possible, he hoped, that this Tiger might not be latched onto *Göring* like the others.

His thoughts were now tempered by his understanding of the likely consequences. They were so different from his initial attempt to escape with the lifeboat. Now he fully understood that his escape, and further participation in the war, would mean changing history. It would affect not only his Luftwaffe friends, but it would likely end the very existence of their families, descendants, and multiple generations of ancestors. He would have a thousand years of blood on his hands. But inaction also meant that generations ahead would be condemned to live under Nazi rule. It was a Nazi rule unencumbered by serious political rivals or human enemies, and now with the advantages of time travel. He knew that he might have to put thoughts of escape out of his mind. But he also knew that they could never be entirely gone.

Then the hatch closed again and he understood why these hopes would have been for naught anyway. The rechner would never have opened it for him if there were a chance he could escape. Then the reason became obvious when he entered. The interior was bare. Even the cargo pod had been removed, exposing the bare weapons module that McHenry had previously only seen in pictures and diagrams. Bamberg and Sanchez were floating in the middle cabin with coffee containers in their hands.

"Isn't this your nap period?" asked Sanchez.

"I couldn't sleep," McHenry answered. He couldn't be sure whether Sanchez was joking or not. "How much are they taking out?"

"The engines came out fast," said Sanchez. "The robots are outside, realigning the unterkarbon. They will be doing that for weeks."

"You look unhappy tonight," observed Bamberg. "Was it more trouble with the SS?"

"You guessed it."

"Let's get you a cup of coffee," said Sanchez, leading the way into the cockpit, which McHenry could see was now configured for a lone pilot seat. Other than that, the cockpit was unchanged, but McHenry could detect a slight hum. The dome showed the outside, including the unterkarbon, which was not normally displayed. Small bug-like robots hugged sections of its webbing. He suddenly realized how rare it is to hear a superfluous sound generated by technology. *Göring* and its Tigers had so few mechanical noises other than those beeps, tones, chimes and alarms designed with the intent of being heard by someone.

"That noise you hear is the auxiliary reactor," explained Bamberg while rearranging the seating. "We would normally not hear it but it is misaligned for testing. Some of the covers are off."

"It's still pretty darn quiet to me," said McHenry.

"Compared to your old aircraft, I am sure that it is," said Bamberg.

McHenry smiled slightly. "Yes, those things are loud." Then the smile lapsed. "Are they still holding Otto Barr?"

"No," said Bamberg. "We were told he is transferring to ship's navigation until further notice. We assume he saw something sensitive and cannot risk being captured."

"Do you think he might have peeked at the Tiger's SS equipment?"

"The side-panel? He would not do that," said Bamberg, shaking his head.

"His SS officer isn't listed on the flight schedule anymore either," added Sanchez. "Whatever it is, it seems to affect both of them." She handed him a container of coffee and then seated herself sideways where she could watch the door. "So," she said. "Tell us what the SS did now. Was it Dale again?"

"Yes, but mostly Stern." Then he thought further. "Actually, it's everything. I got an idea earlier that they rejected the mission because my friend is a Christian."

"They would not like that," said Sanchez. "But I very much doubt that's the only reason."

"It's not," said McHenry. "I'm sure of that much. Stern led me to believe there's something else. He wouldn't say what, but whatever it is, he's not saying."

"I would not expect him to," said Bamberg.

"It is suspicious. I wonder if it could be related to the reason Barr is being held."

"Doubtful," said Sanchez. "I think it's more widespread than one issue. The SS is very busy now. We will have a full flight schedule tomorrow. Don't ask why; they aren't telling us. But don't worry about Otto. I'm sure he's comfortable."

"What can you tell me about the Jews?" He didn't want to change the subject, but her mention of secrecy made him think of it.

"You mean of your time?" asked Bamberg, surprised. He followed up without waiting for an answer. "You must know better than we that no one liked the Jews in your day. This is your time period, after all."

"How many do you think were killed?"

"Killed?" asked Bamberg, surprised. "By whom?"

"That's just it. They're killing millions of Jews."

"Typhus killed a lot of them," said Sanchez. "This was common back then."

"Yes," said Bamberg. "But you said 'killing.' I do not doubt that there were also some executions. Some people were cruel in your time, if you don't mind me saying so. But millions of executions? Millions?"

"Stern admitted it to me."

"It is the first time I had heard of that," said Bamberg.

"That doesn't disturb you?"

"Of course it disturbs us," said Bamberg. "But this happened many generations before we were born. There are many things they cannot tell us."

"Those were cruel times," said Sanchez. "And perhaps that's why it is a secret."

"Even after the war is over?" McHenry asked. "Even after a thousand years?"

"Our society values order," said Bamberg. "How much do you value five hundred years of peace among humankind?"

"I don't know," McHenry said. "Maybe it's not so much the hundreds of years that I'm concerned about. I'm starting to understand that we really are talking about an eternity."

*

McHenry's room seemed eerily quiet when he returned. The music was off, which was fine, but in his weird state of sleepiness, even his own thoughts sounded distant and hollow. It was to be expected, he consoled himself. It was five in the morning. He instructed the rechner to let him sleep until ten.

"You have one event scheduled," the machine responded. A message box overlaid the fake window reminding him of Hitler's birthday rally at nine.

"Tell Hitler I said happy birthday," he whispered, dropping himself into the bed and kicking off his boots.

The machine said nothing.

McHenry snickered. He wondered if the rechner was going to wake him in time for the SS festivities, or whether it would let him sleep until ten. It would really feel good if they do try to wake him early. A fight was just what he needed.

He reached around for the tablet but it wasn't there. He had left it somewhere in SS section, and now considered having the machine create another one. But he needed to sleep. That much was certain, he thought, even if he didn't know whether he'd be getting up at ten or eight thirty. He looked up at the window. The message box was gone.

His thoughts wandered. He was very tired, and yet not sleepy at all.

"Rechner," he called. "Wake me up at seven thirty." He needed to go, he decided, reminding himself that he was an American soldier. A tired American soldier who couldn't sleep.

McHenry was tired. He felt almost drunk. He kept thinking about Adolf Hitler, the man who began World War II, and then ended it with such a grand gesture. Dale had accused him of cultural prejudice, and he had to admit some of it was true. The Nazis were his enemy. Now they wanted to be his friends. It might have worked if they promised to rescue his friend, but they didn't. Even so, he'd have accepted this if he wasn't so certain there was something they were holding back. Hitler's grand gesture meant little to him now.

It had taken a few seconds to remember Parker's name. He wondered why, but was too tired to think. He grew more tired and even less able to sleep.

The door chime sounded.

"One second!" he shouted, jumping clumsily off the bed, and turning it back into a chair. The doors were soundproof, but he also knew the material would sometimes let his voice carry. Such were the properties of its construction, and that ubiquitous rechner's control over them.

McHenry felt the blood drain from his head, but he did his best to stand straight and make himself presentable. "Come in," he said. It was the doctor.

"You should sit down, Herr McHenry," Dr. Evers said, waving a medical wand over McHenry's head.

"Is something wrong?" McHenry asked. He was glad to have any reason to get off his feet, but stressed over the doctor's sudden visit.

A scan of McHenry's brain appeared on the window panel. The doctor studied it for a moment before speaking. "No," he said. "There is nothing wrong. You have been spending much time on the Tigers, have you not?"

"Yes," he replied, watching the colors deepen on the image as he formed the words. "I practice flying there, using the simulator mode."

"And you have been drinking coffee on them, haven't you? A lot of coffee?"

"Of course," he said. "I ate food there too. I thought we could eat anything we wanted."

"Yes," the doctor said, nodding. "That would be okay for everyone else. You are different. Your body is still acclimating to its new potential. It needs to be monitored. The rechner knows what you consume on *Göring*, but not on the Tigers."

McHenry tried to force himself to become more alert. He turned away from the display of his mental faculties in action. The feedback made him uncomfortable. "Is that why I can't sleep?"

"No. You cannot sleep because your brain no longer requires it every day."

"Then why am I not completely awake?"

The doctor looked at his eyes and then turned back to the display. "I do not think you would understand, Herr McHenry. It would be better if you became alert first. Stare at the panel."

McHenry warily complied. The panel showed a different image this time. It was a pattern of intersecting lines.

"*Blitz!*" the doctor commanded, and a flash lit the room.

It was a bright flash. The image stayed in his eyes for a while as they adjusted back to the regular brightness of the room. McHenry was still momentarily confused. It was as though he was just waking up.

"Does this mean I won't ever need to sleep again?"

*

CHAPTER 17

"Not only fortune, but also reputation is always shifting during a war between great men and nations. It is therefore difficult, perhaps even impossible, to determine the political and military importance of individual events in the midst of war. What yesterday seemed a brilliant move can within several weeks or months prove a major mistake, and that which seemed short-sighted and mistaken can later become a decision of deep wisdom."
— *Joseph Goebbels, Speech on Hitler's 55th Birthday, (April 20, 1944)*

Thursday, April 20, 1944

Not needing sleep for another two days, McHenry returned to the hatchway with the disabled Tiger. The pilots were gone. He spent the rest of the early morning watching the airframes crew removing, rebuilding, reinstalling and testing. He stayed out of their way when necessary, asked questions when he had them, and assisted when possible.

He had breakfast at the pilots' mess, discussed the day's activities, and then returned to his quarters to prepare for the event.

The machine's main dispensing drawer slid open when McHenry returned to his room. It was his new suit, as Dale had ordered the previous day.

There were no surprises, which was interesting in its own way. The suit went on just like the Luftwaffe-styled one he had been wearing, pulling the shirt over his head. It tightened by itself. The boots were dark blue. They matched a pattern on his shirt but were otherwise unremarkable.

"Rechner," he ordered. "Display a mirror for me."

He had never worn a tuxedo before, or the mess dress Army uniform for evening wear, and imagined this to be the future Reich's version. The suit had a mildly gaudy flair, but it was something he could live with. He was glad the yellow trim was understated. But how would he look beside all the uniformed men and women at the event? And what did they really want him there for? He could not help but feel he was a trophy. He did not want to be a symbol of the Reich's power.

An image flared into his mind: He was a black man from a nation still repressing even the finest men of his race. The Reich had evolved past its racism, and they were clearly proud of that. Could it be that he was to be a symbol of their evolution? Or could he be a symbol of their *goodness*? To McHenry's mind, that would be even worse. He was still at war, no matter what the Reich thought, and now he might be used as an instrument of propaganda.

He looked down at the Luftwaffe boots lying on the floor beside the new boots on his feet. Clearly, their machine could create anything.

"Rechner," he ordered. "I want a U.S. Army dress uniform. Add rank, medals and wings in accordance with my service record." He pulled off his boots quickly. He didn't want to be late.

*

He could hear singing in the distance as soon as the elevator doors opened. It sounded like the entire SS regiment. Their song was familiar. It was a Nazi song from the era. He had picked up enough German by now to understand a few of the words.

The corridors were empty here. A Luftwaffe man had seen him on the other floor, and his reaction to the dark blue Army dress uniform was a pleasant one. He wasn't wearing a hat. That was a deliberate decision. No one else would be wearing one, and he wouldn't be reflexively tempted to salute.

The large door was open when he arrived, and two SS guards had been ceremoniously posted. The huge main watch room itself was no longer functioning as a watch room. The equipment was gone. The dome was now a blue sky. It was practically a parade ground full of men and women organized in platoons, each facing the raised platform in a circle, and all of them wearing black and silver dress uniforms. McHenry made a quick guess that the hall must have held five hundred.

The two guards were the only ones not singing. Dale had been waiting beside them, resplendent in her SS uniform, pitch black with a shiny black leathery stripe across the front, and a silver swastika on one arm. She stopped singing when she gazed at his American uniform. Her proud smile refused to fade but it looked false and without sincerity. She nodded her head as though approving.

It seemed like she was about to speak but the song ended and the great hall became eerily silent. He looked to the platform in the center where Mtubo stood glaring back at him, with a huge picture of his *Führer*, the august face of Katrina Renard, in the distance behind him. He didn't see a picture of Hitler until he turned to see it behind him.

"I see that our Americaner has decided to dress up for the occasion," Mtubo announced. He then turned to Stern, who was standing on the platform with him, and the two exchanged whispers.

Dale nodded at McHenry and moved formally toward a formation of SS men and women near the center, some of whom he recognized. Her steps were formal, like marching but not quite goose-stepping. He followed, adopting the same pace and keeping in step, acutely aware that he was being watched. Everyone was so much larger than he, and he was conspicuous in every way. Yet, he was determined to make America proud, now and in the future, even after his country exists only in his heart.

They had reached their position in the formation, with Dale and McHenry at the far right corner, when a man shouted, "*Achtung!*" And the entire regiment clicked to attention. He recalled his promise to Dale and followed suit, remembering, too, that the Geneva Convention required adherence to military protocol.

Although the speeches were in German, McHenry was able to catch a few words. Stern began the presentation, speaking of their love for science, their love for history, their love for the Reich, their love for Adolf Hitler, and their love for *Führer* Renard. McHenry wondered whether those thoughts might have been influenced by their meeting the night before.

Then Stern spoke of the mission's importance to the Reich, at which point he stepped to the side for Mtubo to continue the rally. And a rally it was. Mtubo went on at length about the perpetual struggle to maintain order within the greatly expanding Reich. The Reich had expanded to many planets, and the SS always acted as the arm of the *Führer*. Stern stood beside him, applauding Mtubo's remarks, and laughing at his jokes — most of which were lost on McHenry.

Then he spoke about the first *Führer*, Adolf Hitler, wistfully recalling the stories they had all learned about the great struggle to unify Germany, leaving an example for the next Führers as they each worked to unify the world.

McHenry turned his head slightly to study the chamber. It seemed even larger than it did the first time he entered. The screens were gone and the dome was black, with the exception of the *Führer's* picture behind Mtubo. He turned slightly to the right, and that's when he saw the picture of Hitler directly opposite that of Renard. For much of the speech, Mtubo had apparently been speaking to it.

Mtubo then raised his arm in a crisp Nazi salute and shouted in a deep and loud voice, *"SIEG!"* — the German word for *victory*. On this cue, the regiment raised their arms and voices in unison, *"HEIL!"* It was a thunderous cry that evoked the raw power of the men and women of the Reich.

Only one man kept quiet, refusing to raise his arm. McHenry felt proudly conspicuous in the huge chamber. It was like in the newsreels. Perhaps they were reenacting a scene from their history, or perhaps Nazis still did this. McHenry couldn't guess.

"SIEG!"

"HEIL!"

"SIEG!"

"HEIL!"

Mtubo took a small step forward after the tumult and, speaking softly in English, said, "I see that our Americaner does not realize that our victory will be his victory, too." Then he smiled thinly at McHenry. "With time, you will understand."

McHenry stood, motionless, resisting the impulse to say anything. He wondered what he was doing here.

The African Nazi didn't focus on McHenry for long. Speaking in German again, the topic returned to Adolf Hitler, his birthday, the Reich and the future.

McHenry then remembered what Dale told him: *The Third Reich will stand for an eternity.* He considered the predictive abilities of their social science, and their time travel, and he knew that her confidence was justified. The Reich can last for an eternity. Only he can stop them. Whatever the cost, whatever the harm, he must escape.

*

CHAPTER 18

"Waiting. That one word describes Wall Street's attitude, in-action. Commonly, stock market folks, especially professional operators, anticipate events — 'discount' them is the market's word for it. But on the eve of the most momentous happening in history, numbness prevails. Stock speculation is dormant. Recessions and recoveries see-saw within narrow range. Indecisiveness is generally expected to rule while uncertainty reigns, meaning until all-out invasion of Europe is launched."
— *B. C. Forbes, financial journalist, (April 23, 1944)*

Sunday, April 23, 1944

After trying different U.S. Army uniform types, McHenry settled on the dark green service uniform suitable for office wear. He added the waist-high field jacket that was currently being tested by General Eisenhower himself. He never resumed wearing the plain Luftwaffe outfit he'd been given before. He was still a lieutenant in the United States Army Air Force. He was determined to look like one.

He also liked having the extra pockets of the jacket. The opportunity to grab something never came around, but McHenry would be prepared. That American uniform would be an ever-present reminder that he was still at war.

With greater intervals between sleep periods, McHenry spent a lot of time in the disabled Tiger. He'd play with the simulation mode when it was working, and when nobody was about. He also made himself aware of any changes to the projected completion date. The moment the ship was flyable, he wanted to be on it. When crewmen were back at repairs, he'd continue to watch and to help out. He was determined to learn everything he could.

"*Kneifzange*," a crewman called out, holding his hand up in the Tiger's middle cabin.

By now, McHenry knew the word. He reached for the pincers before the man's assistant could get there and handed them to the man.

The crewman, apparently of Asian origin, nodded appreciatively. He used the pincers to pull out the pipe.

His handling seemed rough to McHenry, surprisingly so on such a sophisticated system. He had yet to understand why some things must be handled gingerly, sometimes only by machines, while other things can be treated like the wheels on an old '27 Ford.

The pipe slid out slowly. Finally, both ends floated loosely in the middle cabin.

The crewman put the tool back into the toolbox, and a ring changed color from red to gold. All tools were accounted for. The box sealed shut.

"Thank you again, Herr McHenry," the senior crewman said. He then turned, snapping against a bulkhead when he saw Dale floating at the Tiger hatch in her SS uniform. "*Achtung!*" he shouted to his assistant.

She replied in German, floating to one side as the two men quickly made their way out through the hatch, taking the long pipe out with them.

Their rapid change in demeanor was startling to McHenry. There were few women in his Army, and fewer still who were officers of a rank equivalent to Dale.

"It's getting late for that, you know," she said when they'd gone.

"For what?" he asked.

"That uniform. It will be a thousand years old when we go back home." She reached over for a moment and touched the metallic wings. They looked and felt just like the originals but McHenry knew them to be made of the Reich's advanced materials just like everything else around him.

"Well, nine hundred, anyway," she continued. "Whatever your sentiments — and I do understand them; we all understand them —

I don't think you will want to be wearing it too long after we leave this time. You have the rest of your life to look forward to."

"The crew seems to like it," McHenry said. He reached for the controls, adjusting the view mode as they maneuvered themselves into seats. He wanted the unenhanced view.

"The Luftwaffe crewmembers are military men. They can appreciate your sense of duty even if it is to the wrong side. And, truth be told, that's a big reason why you're here. Your presence is a very pleasant distraction. You have to consider, this was planned as a five-year mission — even if it is ending early. The presence of visitors was going to..."

"Wait a minute," he interrupted. "It's ending early? This is the first I've heard of it."

"It was announced early this morning. Are you still taking naps?"

"That explains it. The doctor says I'll have a few more." He looked up at the maintenance schedule on the panel. He knew that escape was practically impossible, but he hoped that, given sufficient time, an opportunity would eventually come along. "When is this ship leaving?"

"In another month. We will be here long enough to witness the invasion."

"Good," he said sarcastically. "I'll get to see how it is that the entire population can change their minds overnight about fighting the war."

"Oh, Sam," she sighed. "How closely have you been keeping up with events down there?"

"I read the paper every day," he said. "President Roosevelt is still on vacation."

"You're keeping up with where he goes?" She laughed. "I suppose you want to know his location in case you get a chance to escape. Are you planning to land this Tiger on the White House lawn?"

"Maybe," he replied, returning a smile, but wishing his dreams weren't so obvious.

"Have you noticed the strike news?" she asked.

"Airstrikes?" he asked, wondering if she was changing the subject.

"No. I meant the labor strikes in America and Britain."

"I read that. I didn't dwell on it." McHenry shifted uncomfortably in the high seat. "It's unfortunate but these things happen in a free country. It doesn't mean they won't supply us in the end."

"Think about it, Sam. Your country is at war, but you should see that not everyone feels that way. While you were fighting overseas, Americans back home were going on strike. It's worse in England. This will be their worst strike year since the nineteen twenties."

"I'd wager that practically all those workers want the Allies to win. You know the invasion fails partly because of weather. It does not fail because of inadequate matériel."

"No, it doesn't. But the people will be happy to see the war over. That's all I'm saying. They want to get back to their lives."

"They still want us to win. I don't doubt that we would get supplied."

"You miss the point, Sam. This isn't simply a supply issue. You know that human sentiment, morale and propaganda are key ingredients in a war. These same things happened in Germany during the first world war. They had a munitions strike in 1918. It didn't last long enough to have a direct military effect on supply to the front. As a great man observed, *'the moral damage was much more terrible. In the first place, what was the army fighting for if the people at home did not wish it to be victorious? For whom then were these enormous sacrifices and privations being made and endured? Must the soldiers fight for victory while the home front goes on strike against it?*

"'In the second place, what effect did this move have on the enemy?' It made the English and the French more confident that the war might end in their victory — if only they stay in the fight just a little bit longer. *'Here the resistance had lost all the character of an army fighting for a lost cause. In its place there was now a grim determination to struggle through to victory.'*

"And most importantly," she concluded, "they never needed to seek peace as long as Germans showed weakness. They never needed to invade Germany to end that war. The German people of 1918 simply gave up. They wanted peace more than the Allies did. And the Allies knew it. The Kaiser had no choice but to abdicate."

"Were you quoting Coughlin again?" McHenry sniped.

"No. Most of that was Adolf Hitler." She grinned. "My point, Sam, is that it's understandable that people will want to stop the war. I'm not saying that it's always good. It wasn't good for Germany in 1918. They needed a leader to continue to rally the people. The Kaiser was no longer capable of that."

"Oh," he mused. "I'm beginning to understand now."

She looked down at him, smiling.

"What you really don't respect about America is that we would give up."

Her smile disappeared. She reflected on that for a moment. He did, too. It hit both of them hard. To McHenry, giving up bordered on the dishonorable. An outright defeat would be better than giving up when the entire future of the human race is at stake.

It was Dale who spoke again first. "Sam," she said. "Hitler offered far, far better terms than what the Germans received after the first world war. They were really quite contrite. Sometimes peace is the best option."

"Was there really peace after the U.S. and Britain gave up?" McHenry asked resentfully. "Or was this peace only for us while the rest of the world was torn apart?"

"Sometimes the people just need a rest," she said quietly.

He took that non-answer for what it was. "Have you considered trying this with the Grauen?"

"We still remember the Treaty of Versailles," she said, her confidence returning.

"Another treaty that Hitler broke."

"That treaty deserved to be broken," she said firmly.

Then her tone changed, making it obvious to him that she was quoting again. "*Who therefore entertain the thought that the Treaty of Versailles would be honored by all its participants? Does not the vast majority of historians regard that treaty as an unjust document? Was not its chief objective the dismemberment of the German Empire? Did it not impose a fine of 57 billion dollars payable in gold upon a penniless people from whose treasuries had been removed the last ounce of gold? Did it not shackle the German people to the pillar of oppression when it virtually forbade them to trade with other nations? Did it not despoil Germany of all her colonies? And in a spirit of revenge and barbarism, instead of peace and humanity, was not the Treaty of Versailles instrumental in removing more than a million milk cows upon which depended the little children for their food?'*

She was reciting the words more passionately now, *"'Certainly, Germany signed the Treaty of Versailles — because there was no alternative — a treaty that will go down in history as the most inhuman aggression ever committed against any people in the entire history of the civilized world. An aggression which was not aimed at the Kaiser, and at those who were responsible for Germany's participation in the World War. A treaty that was not aimed at the international bankers who sent the Bolsheviks into Russia, but aimed at the poor, victimized people who had remained behind when the malefactors had fled to safety.'*

"And that," she asserted, "was Coughlin."

"Okay, okay," he said. He had already known the treaty was bad one. He regretted bringing it up. "I'll concede that treaty was too heavy-handed. But that doesn't mean I like Hitler or Coughlin."

She smiled, thinking that this was a victory over him. But out of the corner of his eye, he saw the maintenance schedule for the Tiger. It would be fully operational again before the end of May.

Bamberg came in just as Dale was leaving. She greeted him, and looked beyond, perhaps hoping someone else was there, too.

"I'll see you tomorrow for our regular lunch," she said. "I will leave you boys to your pilot talk."

Bamberg gave a polite greeting, and then waited until the hatch had sealed behind her.

"I told you," he said. "They like to be ideological."

*

CHAPTER 19

MONTE CASSINO FALLS TO THE ALLIES

The Polish flag is flying over the ruins of the ancient Italian monastery which has been a symbol of German resistance since the beginning of the year.

Polish troops entered the hill-top abbey this morning, six days after the latest attacks began on this strategic stronghold at the western end of the German defensive position known as the Gustav Line.

British troops have taken control of the fortified town of Cassino at the foot of the "Monastery Hill".

The Allies' hard-fought victory comes four months after their first assault on Monastery Hill failed in January...
— BBC news, (May 18, 1944)

Thursday, May 18, 1944

Reading in his chair, McHenry learned the news that morning feeling momentary joy mixed with sadness. The weeks had gone by. He had never escaped, and Parker was now dead. The Allies were still advancing, oblivious to the sad end that awaited them.

The good news was that Monte Cassino had been taken. Better still, his squadron had been part of it, earning a second Distinguished Unit Citation. But that victory would be for nothing, he knew. He put the tablet down. *They'd been doing so well*, he thought for the hundredth time. The Allies' Italian campaign was moving forward. It didn't make sense that one defeat, even a major defeat such as the invasion would prove to be, could turn the entire war.

It didn't have to. What if he could somehow prevent President Roosevelt's stroke? The Tigers have a first aid kit, he knew. More than that, of course. The lifeboat must have one, too. The future

Nazi medicine could sustain a man indefinitely. President Roosevelt could serve as many terms as necessary to win the war.

It was a dream, McHenry acknowledged to himself. He allowed himself the pleasure of the speculation. Escape was next to impossible. Landing the escape pod in Washington without being shot down by *Göring* was just as unlikely.

Of course, he realized, it would be better to save the Allies' invasion of France. Roosevelt might not even have his stroke if the invasion went well, killing two birds with one stone. A single well-timed burst from a Tiger's energy weapon could do that. The troops would then wade ashore unopposed. Or, better still, destroy Hitler's headquarters in Berlin. One Tiger could well destroy the entire city....

But it was a dream. The *Kommandant* would surely risk detection by the Grauen, and even risk tampering with history itself if McHenry's crusade was going to shatter that history anyway. Clearly, subtlety was required. Subtlety in the extreme.

"Rechner," he called out, thinking of an idea. "Where is Vice President Wallace right now?" He picked up his tablet and saw a map appear with a text description in English. As expected, Wallace was in Washington. More interesting still, he was preparing for an official trip to Russia and China via Alaska. McHenry was intrigued by that. Much of his trip, maybe all of it, would be out of *Göring's* line of sight. If he could get that far, they would not be able to track him immediately. They would need to send Tigers to check their satellites. And one of those Tigers is still out of commission. McHenry smiled. One impossible problem down. Just two impossible problems left to go: Getting out of the ship, and getting away without being blown out of space.

The smile faded a bit. It was still a nice dream, but unlikely. He'd best get back to work.

He wondered what he could do here. If escape is impossible, then how can he destroy the Reich from here? He was already on the most powerful ship in the solar system. Why would he want to leave?

*

He crawled into the Tiger expecting to see technicians still plodding through the hardware. The cables were mostly gone except for one that ran along the floor and terminated at a plug. The back cabin was still empty. He knew that this meant the F-7 main energy weapon was still out but he surmised that the engines must have been sealed back in place ahead of schedule. The SS may be in a fluster but the Luftwaffe mechs were on top of things.

The cockpit dome had one difference: The SS side-panel was open. This wasn't unusual for a ship returning from a mission. The few times McHenry had looked into a side-panel, they had already been cleared. They only presented a simple array of functions that were already available on the main controls. McHenry immediately thought of Barr, and wondered, *could it be that this one wasn't cleared?* He hoped against hope that some remnant of the last mission might remain.

He peered in, seeing almost immediately why the side-panel was open. The crew had been using it to organize the maintenance schedule. He continued looking anyway. There was still a chance that something could be left over.

The first page of the side-panel's display looked promising. Some of it, like sensors and communications, was a duplicate of options he knew were on the Tiger's main panel, and could be projected onto the dome itself. He understood the communications panels all too well, having tried to access them the first chance he was alone. He gathered that the Tiger, while joined to *Göring*, was under something like a Faraday cage, which prevents the emission of any radio signals.

The side-panel was also designed for quick access to an information library. He could see that it tied into the navigation system. Nothing new for him there.

Stepping back in the options tables, he found something else that turned into a dead end. Finally, he came back to the first page, and wound his way back into the maintenance schedule where he first found it.

McHenry was not willing to give up. He compared the main items in the schedule with those listed on the dome, hoping to find a disparity. But there were none. Compared to the options on the main dome, the side-panel's organization layout was surprisingly easy to follow. Airframes, sensors, communications, life support and the unterkarbon net were all marked in green. He stepped down several levels, past several tests that had been checked off.

But, elsewhere, there was so much work left to be done. Weapons, engines and the storage bay were all marked red as still in repair. A quick view revealed that the main energy weapons were still out. There was a long list of things to do, much of it, he knew, were at *Göring's* thirtieth-century equivalent of a machine shop. There was a bigger surprise on the engine schedule page. It was the surprise that would change everything.

The first level of the maintenance checklist was red, but everything below that showed mostly green. The only items in red revealed they were awaiting a long series of inspections, followed by a high-power engine test, and then a test flight. He had to do a double-take. *The actual repairs had already been made.*

As best as he could tell, with his limited understanding of German technical language, this Tiger was probably able to fly. It was down only administratively. It made no sense that their bureaucracy worked this way, but he wasn't going to think about it any further. This was his only chance. He would take it without further thought.

He quickly started the inner banks of engines. This, too, was nothing out of the ordinary. He had seen them do this on low power turns without closing any of the doors. The Tigers were designed to mask their energy output to avoid detection. He just needed to hope nobody tried opening the doors before he could get away.

He unstrapped himself, whirled around, kicked himself through to the main cabin, and took a look around to verify he was alone, and that the door was sealed. Then, swiftly, he pushed himself back.

McHenry was supposed to wait for all the indicators to turn green, but he knew he didn't have time to do this the regulation way he had been taught. They must have some leeway, he reasoned. Once he lights the outer banks, *Göring* would pick up on this quickly. He would hold that off until the end. Checking the unterkarbon net status, he could see that the Tiger's net was wrapped around the side of the ship facing space. The side against the ship would naturally be exposed to detection by *Göring*. He needed to pull away while turning the visible side so as to become invisible to them all as quickly as possible, jinking constantly until he could be sure he was completely cloaked. That would be a lot to do at one time. The indicators were now eighty percent green. That was enough, he decided.

All at once, he reached for the outer door controls, sealed them, and started the main banks. He didn't wait for a reaction from *Göring*. The Tiger pulled away at top speed while he spun and jinked, and jinked again. The unterkarbon net sealed. He jinked again. *Göring* itself became invisible to sensors as the distance increased. That implied he was also out of *Göring's* sensor range. Was he really safe? He jinked again.

Göring became visible again for a brief moment when it released a shower of fire. They were trying to kill him, as he knew they must. He jinked yet again, and then ten more times, but always increasing the distance between them. There was another shower of fire but it was so far off that even the spray of energy could not reveal the massive ship.

"I'm sorry," he said to no one in particular. "I am a soldier."

Now, it was time to take it down.

He inventoried his weapons, what few there were. But it wouldn't matter. Fighting *Göring* directly would be madness. His only chance was to keep them thinking that they could catch him in time to contain the damage to the timeline. Once all hope is lost, and their timeline is irrecoverable, there is no telling what they would do. McHenry wondered momentarily about that. *They must have a contingency plan,* he thought. *How long will they simply sit back and watch as they've been doing? Would they contact today's Berlin and offer their ship, crew, and technology to Hitler? Or does Mtubo just take over and become the new Führer? That would be ironic.*

And what would the Grauen be doing in the meantime? He briefly considered seeking them out, and forming an alliance, but what would their reaction be? Just because they're at war with the Reich doesn't mean they'd be friends with the United States. But this wasn't his decision to make. He had his oath as an Army officer. This should only be for President Roosevelt to decide. *But what if he can't get to the President?*

Either way, his lone Tiger would be outnumbered. He thought he had a better plan, but it was chancy. He needed to get down to Earth.

He worked the navigation panel to plan his descent, a job he could never have done with his old slide-rule. It would be a direct path until touching atmosphere, at which point he knew detection will become possible until he slowed sufficiently that the Tiger could absorb the heat. He would be jinking again, but only a little bit, and then turning again into his destination.

*

Alarms rang throughout the *Göring*. The men and women in *Kontrolle* performed like clockwork. Two panes appeared on the lower section of the dome displaying Mtubo and Stern.

"Prepare to launch the ready-alert Tiger," ordered the *Kommandant*.

"Have you lost him?" shouted Mtubo on the screen.

"Yes," she replied, speaking coolly under the circumstances. "I am ordering a Tiger to defend Berlin in the event that the American thinks he can do something stupid. We will send the remaining Tiger to recover or destroy the one that was stolen as soon as we know where it is."

"Do not destroy it," Mtubo ordered. "We will want it back for Operation Spartacus. Spartacus is more important than preserving our future."

The dome became silent. The *Kommandant* knew it was a shocking statement for the crew, most whom were not even cleared to know what Spartacus was. "*Herr Oberführer!*" the *Kommandant* cautioned.

Mtubo continued: "You are right, of course, about protecting Berlin. Adolf Hitler must be protected in any possible history. It is a matter of principle. Beyond that, we will need the Tigers. There is no doubt now that Spartacus will proceed as soon as we finish here. That will happen regardless of whether we have three Tigers, or two. What are your plans to locate the Tiger?"

The *Kommandant* took a deep breath. "Eventually, the American will want to land. It is unlikely that he has developed the skills to enter the atmosphere without being detected. We will sight him on reentry first, and plot a likely destination. The pursuit Tiger will then find him on the surface very quickly. They will carry a second crew to bring it home."

*

Kathy Dale stood at attention before the door to Stern's office, waiting, not too patiently. There was no need for her to be there. She could easily make her case over a video screen — even on a secure channel — but she knew that personal visits work best. Older generations are more easily persuaded in face-to-face meetings. It was always that way.

The door opened. "Enter," Stern ordered.

"Excuse me, Herr *Standartenführer*," said Dale, standing before Stern's desk. She remained at attention when the door closed behind her. "I request to join the pursuit mission."

Stern raised an eyebrow. "I do not see how or why," he said. "You were restricted to the ship because of what you know. We see Grauen every day now. For you to be captured alive would be a disaster that the Reich could never recover from."

"Sir, I beg to suggest that, with Spartacus now in the plan, a test of Brücke is more important. There may never be a better time."

"Brücke? You are getting ahead of yourself."

"Sir, assuming that Spartacus succeeds..."

"It *will* succeed, *Sturmbannführer*."

"Yes, sir, of course. *When* Spartacus succeeds, we will not know what shape this ship will be in. We may not have more than one chance to initiate Brücke. Here we have an opportunity to run a small scale test."

Stern looked back to the screen, which now showed Dale's report.

"I found several sections of the history sequence for a proper test."

"This is a very good idea," he said, scrolling through the pages of text and charts. "Still, are there no others who could run this?"

"Sir, I am the only one who has the expertise that is also a flight officer." She didn't smile when she said that, but she wanted to.

*

The pursuit Tiger was configured for four people, two in front, and two behind them.

Bamberg was in the pilot's station, grimly checking its systems while Hamilton strapped into the SS station beside him. Vinson remained floating loosely behind them, waiting for the second SS officer to show.

"Any idea when we're leaving?" asked Bamberg.

"I can't tell. My side-panel is locked at the moment. They must still be deciding how much data we can take with us."

"But you were just in ops. You must know something."

"Only that the rechner suggests he was interested in the American Vice President's trip to Russia and China.

"That is something," said Bamberg, bringing the western hemisphere charts up on the dome. The Tiger's rechner would have the optimum path plotted out when the orders come in, but it was prudent to study the options in advance.

Hamilton looked up from his inactive side-panel. "The American is giving up so much in the hope that he could live as a primitive again."

"Let's not forget," said Bamberg. "He thought from the beginning that he was a prisoner of war. He believed it was his duty to escape."

"On that, any of us would do the same if we were in his boots," said Vinson.

Hamilton shook his head. "Those are two different things. He's escaping from higher civilization back to the primitives. And he's a black man, at that. What duty does he owe those people?"

"He's a nationalist at heart," said a fourth voice. It was Dale, entering the cockpit.

Vinson turned. Their eyes met.

"I thought they pulled your flight status," said Hamilton.

"Special project," she answered cryptically. "*Oberführer* Mtubo and Stern are amending the orders now. You will lead this Tiger because you're senior, but you and Bamberg become the retrieval crew for the other Tiger when we arrive. Vinson and I will stay aboard this one. We will complete the mission while you return to *Göring*."

"That's only fair," Hamilton conceded sarcastically. "You are the two who brought back the American in the first place. It is fitting that you be the ones who terminate him."

Although visibly shaken, the others remained silent. Hamilton's sleazy grin twisted and faded. Dale revealed nothing. She floated back to the cargo pod and opened the latch, exposing five androids, seemingly inert in their packed positions. They were still wearing the old-style gray SS uniforms, but their relatively small-sized, twentieth-century statures reminded her of McHenry. "How can one primitive man be so much trouble?" she said, thinking out loud.

"We have the launch order!" Bamberg called from the cockpit. Dale snapped the pod closed, spun, and pushed herself forward.

Hamilton was peering up from his side-panel. "We are to scan the Asian continent, and link up with satellites over that hemisphere, if necessary, to locate the American."

*

CHAPTER 20

"Now, no one in his senses regards bombing, or any other operation of war, with anything but disgust. On the other hand, no decent person cares tuppence for the opinion of posterity. And there is something very distasteful in accepting war as an instrument and at the same time wanting to dodge responsibility for its more obviously barbarous features. Pacifism is a tenable position, provided that you are willing to take the consequences. But all talk of 'limiting' or 'humanizing' war is sheer humbug, based on the fact that the average human being never bothers to examine catchwords."
— *George Orwell, (May 19, 1944)*

Friday, May 19, 1944

Pounding into the atmosphere, this was the first time McHenry could physically feel the hull's vibration within the Tiger. This was a surprise. The simulations had never hinted at this. He fell back on his earlier training in Tuskegee, where he had learned to trust his instruments, and they looked good. This was the first time he could sense that he was moving— even a little bit — and that felt good.

But he didn't know that the ship could take it. He worried about the unterkarbon net, known as it was for being fragile. For the first time, he thought more seriously about the lack of a full test. The Luftwaffe must have had these inspection and test protocols for a good reason. At this point, the only thing he could do was hold on and pray.

A heat dissipation warning appeared on the forward dome's alert panel. *Göring* could detect him now, he knew. *No matter*, he thought. A seasoned Tiger pilot could have avoided this but he didn't have time for a full pre-atmospheric braking. Besides, he was counting on being sighted. Once, anyway.

He was passing far above the western United States, heading northwest. More warnings appeared that radio sensors were out while transiting the ionosphere. This was also normal. He'd seen it in every simulation. The picture of the Earth remained the same, the Tiger's rechners using whatever sensors remained to display as much as possible.

He adjusted the dome to display only visuals. This was America at night. It was dark below, and long past midnight. Away from the coasts, there were no lights-out policies, but even the busiest and brightest cities had long gone to sleep. No matter, he needed to see America as a free man again.

He turned on the indicators again. Soon, the warnings disappeared. He let it continue for another full minute on this course. Not being certain how good *Göring's* sensors might be, there could be no taking chances.

Then, after a quick check on the status of his ship, he brought the navigation panel to the top of the dome, and initiated his second set of coordinates. The Tiger's course shifted abruptly southward. He would be landing in Hawaii.

The plan was crazy, he knew. Once in Hawaii, it would be a more difficult trip back to the mainland. But his initial landing would not be picked up by *Göring*. If he was quick enough, his pursuers would need to access a satellite, and that might buy him time to disappear. He had no idea how much time, but it might be his only shot. The only certainty was, he would get caught eventually.

He unlatched the seat, and swung himself around to see the west coast of the United States receding behind him, wondering whether he would ever see it again.

*

At 100 kilometers out, McHenry switched to a telescopic view of the airfield. This was much larger than his base in Italy. He slowed his approach while scanning the hangars with an infrared view, letting the autopilot slowly approach the airfield. He needed an empty hangar large enough to accommodate his Tiger. Finally, he spotted one by a squadron of dual-engine C-47 cargo aircraft.

The base appeared almost like it was abandoned. He slowed his approach to under 1,000 kilometers per hour, and began circling the field. To his left, he saw Pearl Harbor and its Battleship Row, also strangely quiet. A closer scan showed some activity, a man standing watch here and there, and a few cars. But there were very few people. None of the ships were loading, unloading or moving. Then zooming his view back on Hickam Field again, he noticed that none of the aircraft were flying. Finally, he saw some activity at a bomber squadron. It looked like a single B-24 was being preflighted. This was hardly what one would expect in the middle of a war.

It was when searching for the barracks, and trying to see through the walls, that he realized his error and laughed at himself. He'd been staring at the Tiger's night vision for so long that he forgot it was night. There would be very few flight operations at this hour.

Now grinning, he used the Tiger's rechner to bring him back to the C-47 squadron he found.

There were two men on watch here. He held back a few moments to time their pacing, now hovering well above the two-hundred meters needed to maintain invisibility. It was not the Americans he was hiding from. The base radar was never going to detect him, and he had the cloak of night even without the unterkarbon net around him. The real danger was still above.

He began the dive toward the hangar as each man had turned away. A warning sounded. The ground was affecting the unterkarbon's stealth field as the altitude passed below 150 and then 100 meters. The visibility level status turned red, and then an audible alarm spoke in German. He ignored them all. He simply swerved into the hangar, gracefully retracting the newly repaired unterkarbon net as the Tiger entered. The only adjustment needed was to angle sideways to fit into the short hangar. He extended the landing gear at the last second. *The Luftwaffe pilots could not have done better*, he thought. *Test flight completed.*

It was night outside. The view was illuminated by the Tiger's night-vision equipment. McHenry wasn't sure how to get the local time but he estimated sometime between midnight and three o'clock in the morning.

He opened the hatch, and allowed the ladder to extract while enjoying the mild breeze of Hawaiian air. There was a hint of an oil and gasoline smell to it, which he had missed since his capture. He stood for a moment, letting his eyes adjust to the dark.

He thought again of chocks, set the emergency kit down by the ladder, and went about a quick post-flight inspection. Somebody was going to be back for the Tiger, and it would be better for them, and for him, if it was still in good shape. He was at the landing gear when he heard a shout. A soldier on watch came running into the hangar, with a whistle in one hand, and an M1 rifle in the other.

"Easy, soldier," McHenry barked. Then as the man approached, in a more normal tone, he spoke the words he had been planning during the flight. "I am Lieutenant McHenry of the 99th Fighter Squadron. This is a captured aircraft. It is to remain top secret. My presence here is to remain top secret."

The young private lowered his rifle but didn't say anything.

Another private, with a rifle and a flashlight, came running in to meet them.

"I am Lieutenant McHenry, 99th Fighter Squadron," McHenry repeated, stepping away from the landing gear. "This captured aircraft is to remain top secret. My presence here is to remain top secret."

The two men looked to McHenry, then to the smooth shape of the Tiger with its black exterior, back to McHenry, and then back to the Tiger. One of them pointed his flashlight on the subtle gray Luftwaffe markings.

"Wake the duty officer," McHenry ordered. "You are to contact no one else. You are not to use a radio or your phone. You are not to let anyone else discuss my presence by radio or phone. This is top secret."

The soldiers still said nothing. Astounded, shy, or simply disrespectful, McHenry couldn't know. But it didn't matter. This was one of the times when he just didn't care.

"Do you understand me?" McHenry asked firmly. It was more an order than a question.

Finally, the first soldier looked to the other, who nodded, and then looked back to McHenry again. "Yes, sir. We'd better take you to Lt. Donaldson."

The duty office was in a different hangar, a long walk made longer by the fact that his time was limited. McHenry let the first man, Private Williams, lead the way, and then walked briskly in that direction. The other, Private Dalton, followed behind.

A C-47 cargo aircraft was parked inside the main hangar. Even in the faint light, he recognized repair marks indicative of patched-up bullet holes — a reminder that cargo aircraft are valuable targets. *Perfect overseas transport, too.*

Once inside the duty office, Private Dalton went into a back room to wake the lieutenant. The office was spartan. The furniture looked small. It was startling to be again in the company of men about his own height.

McHenry could hear a groggy voice, and then Dalton talking about a Negro officer and a Nazi zeppelin. When he heard that, McHenry made his way through the door.

"That must be a blimp," said the lieutenant. "A zeppelin wouldn't fit into these hangars."

"It's neither," McHenry interrupted. "Look, I don't have time for this. I'm on a top secret mission. Could we speak privately?"

First Lieutenant Donaldson, wearing pilot wings, was blond and tall, like an American version of Vinson but only about McHenry's height rather than in excess of seven feet.

"You apparently had time to pull your aircraft, blimp, or whatever it is, into another squadron's hangar," said Donaldson. He looked as though he was sizing McHenry up as well, scanning up and down at McHenry's immaculate, apparently too-crisply pressed uniform. "Can I see your orders?"

"I don't have any. This is a special circumstance."

Donaldson fixed his eyes on McHenry's pilot wings. "Are you really a pilot?"

"Yes. My name is First Lieutenant Sam McHenry. 99th Fighter Squadron."

"What did you train on? Did you fly the BT-13?"

"Yes, in training." He wondered what Donaldson was getting at.

"What's the service ceiling?"

"What?"

"The service ceiling. You ought to know that one in your sleep."

Now he understood Donaldson's intention. Tuskegee seemed like a lifetime ago now, but those numbers that had been drilled into his head. He recited from memory, "twenty-one thousand, six hundred and fifty feet."

"Yup. You're an Army pilot," Donaldson said more cheerfully.

McHenry relaxed a bit. He was impressed with Donaldson. His plan needed somebody like him, although he didn't want someone so close to where he parked the Tiger. Still, he didn't have much time, and he could do worse in finding help.

Donaldson waved the men outside, and then his face took a more serious tone.

"I believe you're a pilot, and I believe you're an officer. I don't believe any cockamamie story about you being on a secret mission, but I didn't want to argue with you in front of the men. Look at that uniform you're wearing. Nobody outside of Washington irons their shirts that way for a utility uniform unless they've got you serving some generals' coffee."

"I don't care whether you fully believe me or not. You can have my aircraft, for all it will do you, but I don't recommend being too close. The Reich — that is the Nazis — are coming back for it."

"In Hawaii? I hardly think they'll be invading Pearl."

"Think what you like. They'll be here sooner than you think. I only need two things: Assistance getting out of here, and secrecy. You can't inform anyone of my presence by radio or phone."

"That's a no-can-do," said Donaldson. He shook his head and reached for the phone on the desk.

Startled, McHenry jumped for it, yanking the line out of the wall. Donaldson grabbed the base of the phone, and tried to kick McHenry away. Both were quickly on the floor, but McHenry eased back when the two privates came rushing in, Private Dalton aiming the muzzle of his rifle at his face.

"Sit down in that chair!" Donaldson demanded, rising to his feet, and feeling his face for injuries.

McHenry complied. "I didn't want that, but you cannot use the phone. This is more important than you know."

Donaldson grabbed his hat, and looked to Dalton. "Keep an eye on him."

"Don't make any phone calls," McHenry insisted.

"I'm not doing anything until I take a look at your blimp."

"Donaldson!" McHenry called. "There's a radio — of sorts — sitting by the ladder. Bring it back with you."

Donaldson nodded, then gestured to the other private, and the two went outside through the dark hangar.

*

Alone with Private Dalton, McHenry looked up and noticed a clock showing two-forty-five. He regretted the time he'd wasted here, and the additional time before he could get out. Any flights to the States would probably be leaving early in the morning. He knew he only had a few hours.

Dalton lowered his rifle and reached into a wastebasket. He pulled out a newspaper and tossed it to McHenry. "Here's a Negro paper some passenger left behind."

Was he making a subtle racist jab, McHenry wondered, or was that a genuine attempt to be polite? He decided it best to play aloof and disinterested. He looked at the masthead. It was the *Chicago Defender.* "Thank you, Private. I'll look at it later."

Dalton nodded and went to a radio that sat atop a cabinet. It was large, bulky, and primitive-looking to McHenry, now that he'd seen the future. After it warmed up, the soldier turned the knob to find a station broadcasting at this hour.

"I'd like to hear the latest news, if there is any," McHenry said, trying to sound more at ease.

"That's fine with me," he said. Then, thinking better, he added, "Sir." Presently, he found a station reciting sports scores.

McHenry looked back to the clock. It shouldn't have taken so long. He wondered if Donaldson was playing with the controls. It might solve so many problems if the Tiger could just explode.

The voice on the radio was now talking about the war. It was the victory at Monte Cassino again. Nothing new to McHenry. Then the reporter was talking about Germany, playing brief clips of Roosevelt and Churchill. Then he heard Hitler shouting on the radio.

Without thinking, McHenry rose to attention. He quickly realized his *faux pas*, but not quickly enough to avoid generating a look of puzzlement from Dalton. Before he could think of something to say, Donaldson returned, the emergency kit in his hand, and a friendlier look on his face. He ordered Dalton outside.

"Let's start over," he said. "Call me Ward."

McHenry shook the man's outstretched hand, deciding then that it's best to tell the real story. Or, most of the real story. Secrecy would serve him well. "I'm Sam."

"I see the Luftwaffe emblem," said Donaldson. "I know it's not a zeppelin. I know it's not a rocket. What is it, and how did you get it, and why is it here?"

"I'll be frank with you," McHenry said. "I'm not on a secret mission. I just wasn't sure you would believe the whole truth."

"Try it."

"I'll start from the beginning. I am a pilot in the 99th Fighter Squadron. We're in the Mediterranean Theater. I was flying out of Italy."

"I heard about you guys. There's an article about your squadron in that Negro paper. You're a long way from where you're supposed to be."

"I had to ditch into the sea in April. Engine trouble. I would have been killed but I was rescued by Nazis." McHenry paused here, unsure. Was seeing the outside of the Tiger really enough that Donaldson would believe him? He went this far. He might as well say it. "But these Nazis were from the future."

"That's a time machine?" Donaldson laughed, without the slightest pause, having gone in an instant from receptive to skeptical to dismissive. "There won't be Nazis in the future, Sam. The war in Europe will be over by Christmas. We're not going to lose."

"It's worse than losing. We're giving up. They'll get a negotiated settlement."

Donaldson was now going from dismissive to outright angry. "The President will never settle. Those defeatists begging for a peace settlement have already been exposed for what they are. They really don't care about peace at all. Half of them are outright Nazi sympathizers. The other half simply hate the Roosevelt administration."

"Roosevelt will be dead of a stroke in a couple of weeks," McHenry said grimly. But as distressing as Donaldson's disbelief was, McHenry noticed — and appreciated — the anger behind his words. This was a man who could fight, not just now, but in the future when it mattered.

"Vice President Wallace wouldn't settle either," Donaldson said slowly. It was a half-hearted statement but McHenry was still losing him for the moment.

"I'm guessing you didn't go inside the ship."

"I didn't see how to open a hatch. I gave it a long walkaround."

"That's how I got this uniform," McHenry said quickly. He was going to open the emergency kit. The display functions would surely convince anybody, but then he looked again at his uniform. "The material itself looks the same as ours but it's not like the real ones at all. It's tough. It never wrinkles. Coffee stains come right out. I've worn this for a couple of days, and it feels fresh, like I just took it off the clothesline."

Donaldson looked more dismissive.

"Let me show you something," McHenry said. "Let's compare wings." He opened his jacket, reached inside his shirt and pulled the clasps off the pilot wings from his shirt. Donaldson hesitated only for a moment. His eyes noticeably widened when McHenry's shirt stretched so easily. His own shirt had to be unbuttoned in order to pull off his own wings.

"Compare the silver. Try bending mine. You've never seen metal as strong and as light as this," said McHenry, letting Donaldson hold both sets of wings. The normal wings were not that heavy. It was a small piece of metal. But the advanced material of McHenry's wings were so noticeably lighter. He was confident Donaldson would believe it all now.

*

"The American had been detected entering the atmosphere," said Hamilton. "The flight path leads to China."

"That's all?" asked Dale from the back seat.

"This was seventy-five minutes ago," said Hamilton. He detached the satellite connection. "He's invisible again. He may not have made a landing. We will be able to find him when we're closer in."

Bamberg switched the dome from nav to sensor mode. They would be hitting atmosphere soon, and he wanted one more look at the full display. "Who here thinks McHenry is stupid enough not to know the rechner would be picking up on his interest in China?"

"He's a twentieth-century old-timer," Hamilton said. "He doesn't have the intellect of an *Übermensch*."

"He is smarter than you give him credit for," said Vinson from the back seat.

"I saw no evidence of that."

"And yet, he was told, time and time again, that escape was impossible," Bamberg snickered.

"Hamilton," Dale interrupted. "It may be prudent to touch the region's monitoring satellite before we descend any further. It could have observed his landing by now."

Hamilton looked down at his side-panel. "That will waste at least half an hour. We still have a chance to stop him before he alters the future."

"We will waste three hours if we reach China and it turns out he landed in Guam," said Bamberg.

"Or Pearl Harbor," said Dale.

*

Once convinced, Donaldson had taken to understanding the situation immediately. He called the two men on guard duty and had them close the hangar doors. There would be a shift change at 0400, but the men would gladly stay on for the rest of the morning. In this way, the Tiger's presence would remain a close secret. Now, it was time to take it to a higher authority.

"No one senior who might be watched," McHenry cautioned. He hadn't taken the time to detail the full panoply of his experience aboard *Göring* but Donaldson appeared to accept that without question.

"Not a problem," Donaldson replied. He reached into a locker and pulled out two hats, tossing one to McHenry. "My squadron C.O. is with the rest of the squadron that moved west. This detachment is run by a lieutenant colonel. But I do have to tell someone. You can't ask me to keep a hangar closed on my own authority."

McHenry nodded, picked up the emergency kit, and grabbed the newspaper on the way out the door. "For the flight. I'm hoping for a long trip."

"That ship in the hangar can travel through time?" asked Donaldson, once the jeep was in gear.

"No, it's only for normal space, short range. It can make it as far as the other planets. Think of it as a combo C-47 and B-25."

"She's armed?"

"It was just under maintenance. It only has beam weapons right now. That's more deadly than anything we've got but it's small potatoes compared to what it could have, and much less than what the *Göring* has. That's their main ship. But fully armed, these could destroy cities with atomic bombs if they wanted to."

Donaldson looked bewildered.

"Atomic weapons are real, although different than H. G. Wells described."

"It's not that. I just read a story about atomic bombs in *Astounding* last month. Everything seems more real now."

They arrived at the officers' quarters and walked along the sidewalk to a door at the far end.

The lights turned on, a moment after Donaldson knocked. Then the door opened, revealing an unshaven man in his mid-thirties wearing only his underwear.

"May we come in, Colonel?"

Blanding looked over at McHenry, and then back to Donaldson. "No. What do you need?"

"I have a story to tell you, sir."

"Are you giving me a story or just an excuse?"

He motioned Donaldson to come inside. Donaldson looked back at McHenry apologetically.

"I'll be in the jeep, said McHenry sullenly. The fate of the world is at stake, the entire future of mankind, and yet he has to wait for jim crow protocol.

He took the newspaper from the jeep, and stepped toward a lamppost adjacent to the building. It was a fine spot to read, but instead of reading, he realized that he was out in the open. Looking all around him, his mental reflexes came back from when he was flying his P-40. *This would be an easy shot for one of those SS robots*, he realized.

Most likely, he imagined, they would be wearing U.S. Army uniforms. It would be done unobtrusively, so as not to draw attention to themselves, or they would be changing history even more. They might prefer that he's hidden. Then he realized that, when they get within a mile, it'll probably be too late for him to get away. There was no sense worrying about close-quarter combat. He needed to get off the island as fast as possible.

He opened the paper to start reading when Donaldson came out again. Blanding was behind him, fully dressed now, but badly needing a shave.

"Back to the hangar," Donaldson beckoned.

*

Briefing Lt. Col. Blanding might been more difficult than first thought, but he became a different man when he saw the inside of the Tiger. McHenry sat at the controls; Blanding sat beside him; and Donaldson stood behind, just awestruck.

"*Rechner, aufleuchten!*" McHenry ordered the Tiger's rechner. The dome was now displaying the view from inside of the hangar. They could see the night outside beyond as though it was daylight. The two guards, Dalton and Williams, were clearly at their posts whispering to each other. The presence of the hangar doors and walls were noticeable but it was not a barrier to the view of the distance. McHenry knew that, despite the lesser spectacle, for them it must be something like how he felt when he first saw the Earth in *Kontrolle*.

"I've got to hand it to you, Lieutenant," said Blanding. "I don't know how you managed to steal this thing, but you've got to be one brilliant son-of-a-bitch."

"You believe it now, sir?" asked McHenry.

"Why are these seats so big?" asked Blanding.

"They're bigger than we are."

"What kind of ordnance do we have?"

"It's a beam weapon of a sort, but nothing we can use against them, and nothing we can remove. They were finishing an overhaul when I commandeered it." McHenry left it at that. The time was wasting away. He considered saying good-bye, and leaving it all in their hands. But he needed one more thing from them. Something big. McHenry reached toward the control panel. "I'm sorry, sir. We need to get out of here. I don't know how long we've got. I've burned over an hour already, and I still need something from you."

"Hold on a second, son," Blanding interrupted. "Yes, I do believe you. Right now, I'll believe anything you want to say. But this is a strategic asset. I am not just leaving it here for these Krauts."

"The knowledge I have is a strategic asset, sir," McHenry said. "It will be lost as soon as they get me. This ship will be gone soon. There is nothing we can do to stop them from either taking it or blowing it up."

"Colonel Blanding is right, Sam," said Donaldson. "This is just too much to give up. We can win the war right here — with both Germany and Japan."

Exasperated, McHenry shook his head. "No, we can't. *They* won't let us win the war. If we did win the war, they can take over any time they want. They want history to go on exactly as it did for them before. That's the only thing stopping them from doing anything they want to do." After a pause, he corrected himself: "Well, that's almost the only thing."

Eyebrows raised a fraction, the two other men looked over at McHenry.

"Sorry, Ward," McHenry apologized. "You'd better step outside. This is need-to-know."

"What? I'm no...," Donaldson started to protest.

"Nothing personal. This stays compartmentalized. They'll get to us each eventually, and they will find out everything you know. The only chance we have is if one of us survives, and the information is separated."

"Got it," Donaldson acknowledged warily. "I'll be outside." He took one more quick look around the dome, and then stepped toward the door.

"Donaldson, hold on," the colonel called, pulling his keys out of his pocket. "Go to the vests in the lockers. Get your pistol, and then get mine for McHenry."

"Yes, sir," Donaldson said, and then disappeared.

McHenry waited until he could see Donaldson outside on the dome, then held up the emergency kit in his hands. "You'll have to take my word for it that I have good reasons to compartmentalize what I tell each of you. I don't know all their capabilities but I do know that they are more capable than you can imagine. There is something I haven't told you. The Reich has another enemy. They're here. They could tip the balance."

"You mean people on another planet? People that aren't human?"

McHenry nodded. "They call them the Grauen."

"They're potential allies!" The colonel looked at the box McHenry was holding and understood the connection. "What you're thinking is that you have an advanced kind of radio here that can contact these people, creatures, or whatever they are."

McHenry nodded again.

"Doesn't this ship have a radio that could work? Just take this thing up to altitude for a better signal. Why couldn't we just call them right now?"

"With all due respect, sir, you don't have the authority. Nobody on this island does. We don't know that we will like the Grauen any more than the Nazis do. The martian invaders of H. G. Wells had no interest in finding allies. These might be no different. This can only be a decision for President Roosevelt."

"You're right," Blanding admitted slowly, easing his grip on the seat. "We would be gambling the world. The devil we know or the devil we don't know."

"Yes, sir. I'm only guessing that we can send a message on a channel that the Grauen would immediately recognize as out of our time. It might get them curious enough to send a response. But if it works, the Grauen could be worse than the Nazis. From what I've gathered, the Nazis have had almost no interaction with them other than occasional firefights. The men and women on that ship tell me they know very little about them."

The colonel showed visible surprise. "They're carrying passengers?"

McHenry needed a few seconds to understand his meaning. "No, sir," he said. "The women on that ship aren't passengers. They're crew."

Blanding looked like he was stifling a smile.

McHenry stifled his own smile, too. He considered telling him about the woman *Führer*, the woman *Kommandant*, and especially about Mtubo, the black *SS-Oberführer*, but thought it best to keep things simple. Time was running out.

Blanding went back to staring at the dome again, through the back wall of the hangar and beyond. "I'll tell you something I've not thought much about since the attack on Pearl," he said. "I used to like America First, one of the groups that, before Pearl Harbor, had opposed our getting into the war. I wasn't an actual member, you understand. I was a Roosevelt man. But the talk of staying out of the war made sense to me. And I trusted Lindbergh."

"I do understand that, sir," said McHenry.

"And when all the communists changed from being anti-war to pro-war, it only made more sense that we should stay out of it."

"A lot of people felt that way."

"Too many people still do," Blanding snapped. "But not me. I changed my mind on December seventh. And after what I've seen and heard here, I'm never changing it back. I'm in this war even if the rest of the country gives up."

"I'm glad to hear that, sir."

Blanding pulled himself out of the seat. "Okay, Lieutenant. You're the only man who really knows what we're up against. I think I know what you're going to ask for, but this is your mission. You tell me, what's your next step?"

"I need a flight to California," said McHenry, standing up beside him. He was starting to like Blanding's rough charm. He felt bad about having given him the bum story. If there was one thing he took from Dale, it was what she said of the Treaty of Versailles. Calling the Grauen was never going to be part of the real plan.

*

174

Donaldson was waiting at the ramp outside.

"File a flight plan to California and order up some fuel," Blanding ordered. "You're flying co-pilot. We'll get somebody to wake up Taylor for navigator, and one of the mechs for the preflight. I want one who can fly loadmaster. Make this look like a regular flight."

"Can we do this?"

"Nobody's going to worry about the regs when this is over. I'll leave a note for Watkins so that he can keep our stories straight."

Dalton and Williams had pulled the hangar door open enough for a jeep to get through. The jeep had its canvas top on.

"It will give you some cover from anyone looking from overhead," Donaldson explained.

"You just saw they can see through walls," sneered Blanding. "What's that going to do?"

"It's still good, sir," said McHenry, still carrying the emergency kit. "Every little bit helps. A little bit could make just enough of a difference. Just one thing, sir. I need to stay away from here until you're ready to take off, just in case they get here before we're ready."

"Williams!" Blanding shouted. "Hustle over to the B.O.Q. and get Lieutenant Taylor now. Tell him nothing about what happened here, but tell him to get here now. He can get dressed on the way. I'm not kidding either. I want him getting dressed on the way!" Then back to McHenry, "Okay, you stay with Donaldson while he files just in case all hell breaks loose here. But don't you worry. We'll be ready to turn engines by the time you get back."

*

CHAPTER 21

SEDITION TRIAL DEFENDANTS CLAIM
'FREE SPEECH' ISSUE

The Defense in Washington's mass sedition conspiracy trial yesterday laid a basis for making "free speech" the issue upon which to seek acquittal of the 29 defendants.

"Free speech is the paramount issue — the only issue," Lawrence Dennis, a defendant, told the jury.

. . .

Dennis, described by the prosecution as "the Alfred Rosenberg of the (Nazi) movement" in this country, who supplied "ideas" to other defendants, called it a "political trial" and urged the jury "not to blame the defendants, because they didn't ask for it."
— *Associated Press, (May 19, 1944)*

Ground and air crews were about, heading for early preflights, as Donaldson pulled the jeep into the parking lot at the tower. "I'll make it quick. I don't think Blanding's going to mind if I fudge some details."

They were parked near a streetlamp. McHenry pulled out the *Chicago Defender* after a few minutes of waiting. As Donaldson had said, there was an article about the 99th. It was right on the second page.

TWO 99TH PILOTS BACK IN U.S.

That was them. As the sole black fighter squadron, the Tuskegee airmen were the only "99th" that mattered to readers of the *Defender*. But even before starting to read the story, McHenry's heart leaped when he spotted the name Capt. Joseph C. Parker in the first paragraph. Expecting it to say something else, he read the words without comprehending. He read the entire paragraph again slowly to be sure he hadn't misunderstood the context.

Parker was alive! There was no mistaking it. The article said he was reassigned, and back in the United States, having completed his combat deployment in North Africa and Italy. It even quoted him at a redistribution station in Atlantic City.

Confused, grateful, angry, and teary-eyed, he immediately believed he had been the victim of a cruel lie. But after reading the paragraph once again, and thinking it through, he knew it could only mean one thing: For the Reich, history had changed from the time that *Göring* had left the thirtieth-century. The change may be minor, to be sure, but it could only be catastrophic for the crew aboard *Göring*.

The implications raced through his mind. If he had stumbled across this one discrepancy, he wondered how many other changes there could be. It explained a lot about the recent secrecy. Most of all, a weight was off his conscience. Whatever he does now to change the course of future history, it could not affect the men and women aboard *Göring*. That die had already been cast by someone else.

But he could not understand how this could happen. If nothing else, he trusted the professionalism of *Göring's* crew. They were meticulous. Something else must have happened. Something big.

Donaldson came back flashing a thumbs up. McHenry waved that off. "There's a monkey-wrench in the works."

"Serious?"

"It is serious for them. I have no idea how it affects us."

He flattened out the page of the newspaper and held it up to Donaldson. "See here? I know this man. He's my friend. I looked him up on this machine they have, telling what happens to everybody. He was listed as being killed in action last month."

"But it's a common name. Could there be two?"

"Not without me knowing about it. This is him."

Donaldson lifted his hands. "Well, either this paper's wrong or your Nazis lied to you."

"They had no reason to lie to me," McHenry said. "Not about something like this, anyway."

"Could it be some kind of trick for interrogation?"

"I wasn't interrogated. They already know everything there is to know."

"Then *they* must have done something."

"They're too careful. They don't want history changing. Otherwise, there won't be a home to go back to."

"Irregardless, your escape couldn't have changed this. This happened last week," Donaldson said, pointing to the paper. "Somebody else must have changed something before you left."

"Yes," McHenry agreed. Someone. *Was it the Grauen?* he wondered. *Or someone aboard the Göring? But why? And how?* He couldn't imagine.

*

Private Williams was standing his post at the well-lit hangar entrance when he saw the two white-uniformed naval officers arrive on foot. He carried a flare gun now, having had to give the rifle to the man who came to relieve him at the end of his watch. He fidgeted with the flare more nervously when he spotted the gold braid on one of the officer's hats. He stood crisply at attention, saluted, and warned the men to halt.

"Who is in charge here?" asked one of the men.

Blanding rushed out the hangar's side exit, saluting the senior officer. "I'm in charge, Commander," he said. He cast a confident eye to Williams, not to reassure him, but to strengthen his resolve. "My name's Blanding."

"I'm Commander Harrington of Navy Special Projects," the man replied, sharply returning the salute. "We've had a secret aircraft stolen. We believe you have it in your hangar."

Blanding appeared surprised. "We weren't told it belonged to the Navy."

"I sure hope you didn't believe the crazy Negro who stole it," said Harrington, now grinning.

"He's a lot smarter than you would think," said the man beside him.

"That, I don't doubt," said Blanding. "He had me completely fooled." Blanding could see Harrington's grin transform into the smile of a salesman, strangely reminding him of a movie character. They both reminded him of movie characters. The crispness of their uniforms just added to the odd manner about the men.

"You see, we need to recover this experimental aircraft. We also need to find the thief. He's carrying classified documents, you understand. Time is of the essence. Do you know where he could be found?"

"Better than that. I can take you right to him." And with that, Blanding reached for his own flare gun.

*

McHenry and Donaldson both saw the flares at once. First one, and another an instant later. Then more from slightly different locations from the direction of the C-47 flight line.

"Trouble," McHenry murmured.

"I counted five. Colonel Blanding and the men." Donaldson turned the wheel sharp, making a three-point-turn, and headed off in the opposite direction. "They're sending us a warning."

"Your colonel is a good man."

"That he is," said Donaldson. He made a sharp right turn at the next corner.

"Where are you going?"

"I saw a bomber on the flight schedule when I was at the tower. It's going to California. I'm getting us on it." Then, after another second, "What do you think will happen to them?"

"Can't be sure," McHenry replied. "If not for history already changing, they would put a high priority on keeping things as they were. That would mean keeping everyone alive — except for me, that is. As it stands now, I can't guess what their plans would be."

"I hate to say this, but whatever you intended to keep secret from me, they'll get it if you think they can make Blanding talk."

McHenry didn't understand.

"It was when you wanted to speak to Blanding in private."

"Oh that. I know. I was counting on it."

It took Donaldson a few seconds to catch on. "It's a ruse? Will it work?"

"I haven't the slightest idea," McHenry conceded.

They pulled into the lot behind the bomber hangars, one of which had its floodlights on. The first lights of dawn were showing in the east.

*

At two kilometers up, Vinson and Dale could watch the recaptured Tiger depart. Its unterkarbon net quickly unfurled, and the Tiger disappeared from view entirely once high enough to avoid ground refraction.

"That was the easy part," Vinson sighed.

Looking down at her side-panel, Dale pretended not to hear what he was implying. "I'm transferring a flight plan to your system. There isn't much time. We need to handle this as soon as we have Sam back."

"Back? You mean you are not killing him?" asked Vinson.

"Hell no!," she said adamantly. "I don't see that we have to."

Relieved, Vinson left that issue aside and studied the chart. He shook his head. "I don't understand. These are for the French province. I thought the mission was to recover Sam, remove any traces of his interactions, and then return to the *Göring*. What does Europe have to do with that?"

He studied her eyes, which revealed nothing.

"I hope I am not stepping out of line."

"It's not that," she said. "We don't yet know what changes he made to the future. He may not have done anything yet of consequence. But whatever he does to our future is insignificant. We'll cover up his tracks if we have time, but we have something more important to do as soon as we're done here."

"Insignificant? Compared to what? Saving our future is the top priority!" Vinson kept his eyes on her, pleading.

"Okay," she said. "You need to know the truth. It's worse than most crew members are aware."

"What could be worse than altering our timeline? It affects our home."

She paused again. This time, Vinson remained quiet while she pondered, peering up at the forward dome.

"I'm afraid that history has already changed," she said. Finally, she turned back to him. "It was only fairly recently that we discovered this. Nothing major — yet. But I don't need to tell you, even a small change can become a major change over the following centuries."

He was stunned.

"The change was not by us," she added.

"Changed by the Grauen?"

She nodded.

"So, the Grauen have time travel," he reflected, still distraught but now also flustered. "How can that happen now? We're in the past. They would have destroyed our own timeline before we were even born."

"It would have, if they had changed history here in our own solar system. But not if they changed their own history. It probably happened at the Grauen homeworld eight-thousand light-years away. Ships from their new timeline came into ours while we were here, or perhaps while we were at the transit point where we went back in time."

Vinson looked her blankly. She knew that he didn't understand.

"Changes in the timeline ripple back at the speed of light," she said.

"The SS had to keep *that* a secret, too?" Vinson stammered.

"That's not strictly an SS secret. The Luftwaffe is aware of this, but it's out of your clearance. It was out of mine, too, until recently."

"When you were off flight status," he concluded. "And that's also why Otto Barr was quarantined."

"Yes. We suspected that the Grauen ship that Barr saw was from the other timeline. We decided that should be kept secret for now."

His mind raced through the implications. Educated in astrophysics since he was a child, and with the training of an interstellar-flight-qualified Luftwaffe pilot, he was still flummoxed. Faster-than-light starships would outrun timeline changes, he realized, assuming one could know it was coming. "It doesn't make sense," he said. "The geometry doesn't work out."

He remained deep in thought until the rechner alerted. He didn't even think to ask how the SS could know where the Grauen homeworld was.

*

Carrying two boxes, Donaldson approached the jeep and tossed one of the boxes to McHenry.

"What's this?"

"It's your box lunch for the flight." Donaldson grinned. "We're in luck. That B-24 is going back to the States this morning. They'll take two more passengers. A friend of mine is flying co-pilot. He's quietly slipping us on the manifest as a favor to me as long as we don't make any waves. They never check whether passengers have orders."

Feeling more at ease at last, McHenry laughed, jumping out of the jeep. "He doesn't think we're on the lam, does he? I don't want him calling the M.P.'s."

"I did have to assure him we're not AWOL. I didn't have to lie. I do have Blanding's authorization."

They made their way around the hangar, and toward the distant aircraft on the tarmac. The mechanics were making their way back inside, pulling a cart behind them. The sun hadn't risen yet, but it was lighter now. It was a slightly foggy morning.

"We've had mornings exactly like this in Italy."

"I haven't seen fog like this since I was in the States," said Donaldson.

McHenry stopped. "Hold on. I wonder if this is natural."

"It's unusual here on the island but I don't know that it's impossible. You really think your Nazis can create fog?"

"You know we can create fog right now. We're talking about people who can manipulate gravity."

"That doesn't mean they brought a fog-making machine down with them."

"Good point. Just the same, it's suspicious." McHenry remained there, looking at the lights around the aircraft two hundred feet ahead, and then to the hangar behind him, still visible, but indistinct. There was an awful lot of fog.

Donaldson looked to McHenry, seeing the concern on his face. "This flight is still our only good option."

"Ward," McHenry said, still hesitating. "It might be a good idea if we split up here."

"Why? My best use to you is helping you get to Washington. I'm not quitting now. I want to win this war."

"I'm not asking you to quit. My best use for *you* now is that you survive." He was speaking more quickly now, certain that he was running out of time. "You're part of the plan. I need for you to survive. This is a longer term strategy than just the next few weeks. The war is much bigger than against Hitler. I need for you to continue even if the President, or the next one, chooses to give up."

"What are you saying? How am I supposed to do that?"

"I don't mean by setting off bombs. Someone has to be able to pick up the pieces, keep the country strong, hold back the waves of defeatism, and resist the return to appeasement. If we do lose here, which I think likely, the rest of the country is going to weaken, and maybe turn on itself."

"I'm just a lieutenant, Sam. You need to tell this to people in Washington."

"You're a lieutenant today. You'll be something else in ten years, and something else again in twenty. You may have the rest of the century to make a difference. *The* difference. Maybe you'll get into politics, or maybe you'll invent or discover something that keeps America on top. This is not only one war. It's this war, and the one after that. Most of all, it's the wars the country is not going to fight, but should, just like the way we didn't get into this one until Hitler took half of Europe. Hitler could have lost everything when he retook the Rhineland in '36 — if only the British and French had threatened war right then. We could have avoided war in Europe entirely, if only we'd been the strong ones. And now we're going right back to appeasement again, here and in the rest of the world. Fascist movements will rise on every continent until they all join the Reich. You have to stop them every chance you get or it's Führers all the way from here on in."

McHenry opened the emergency kit and pulled out a small cartridge. "I know you're just one man, Ward. Maybe this will help."

Donaldson looked the device over. The legend was written in German.

"It's advanced technology," McHenry explained. "Translate the label. You've got years, decades even, to figure out how it works. Heck, you can probably learn something critical just by figuring out what the container is made from."

"Okay, Sam," Donaldson said. He put the device in with the box lunch and held it tight. "But at least let me see you on board that plane. I can't promise to fight the next war without continuing to fight this one." He held out his hand, and the two men shook.

"It's a deal."

They looked toward the B-24, now very hazy in the morning fog, and then back to the hangar. The fog was now so thick that the hangar was no longer visible at all, but they could see two mechanics walking in their direction. Then the B-24 fogged over, too.

"You're right, something's wrong here," said Donaldson.

A form appeared above them out of the mist. McHenry recognized the unterkarbon layers around a Tiger. Donaldson pulled his .45 and fired at the craft.

"No!" McHenry shouted. "It's too late. Get out of here!"

Donaldson emptied the magazine of his pistol, but it was indeed too late. The two mechanics reached them. One grabbed Donaldson's hand, deftly removed the weapon, and then held him in place. The other grabbed McHenry. Both now immobilized, Donaldson was shocked and angry at these men, but McHenry understood what they were. He remembered the name for them.

"You two are *Fallschirmjäger*, aren't you?" he asked. "Robots?"

They said nothing. The Tiger's hatch opened suddenly and a figure stepped out of the mist dressed in a black SS uniform, towering over all of them. It was Dale. She smiled down at McHenry, then coolly to Donaldson, seeming to enjoy the look of shock on his face.

"Whatever he told you about us, you can now see that it's true," she taunted. Then turning to McHenry, she said, "you really shouldn't have done this."

"You know that I had to," McHenry responded.

"Yes, I do. If there is one thing we all agree on, it is duty."

"I know that your future was shot before I left."

"So, you've figured that out," she said, sadly. "But the timeline will be repaired." She stepped down the ladder but was still much taller than either of them. "Anyway, this is bigger than our one future."

Donaldson began struggling visibly. The robot held him tight. "Why does she speak with an American accent?" he blurted out.

Dale stepped beside him and looked down at his eyes. "Because I was born in Chicago." Her gleeful smile returned. "You look like an Aryan version of Sam here. It's a pity we can't bring you back with us. But you need to live your life. And, really, one American soldier is more than enough trouble. Now you've seen too much. Sleep."

Before Donaldson could utter another word, he was unconscious, slumped in the robot's arms.

She looked to McHenry, then to the robot holding him. "Him, too."

*

McHenry didn't recognize where he was when she and Vinson woke him. He guessed correctly that he must be in the Tiger's storage rack. Sensing gravity he guessed, correctly again, that they hadn't yet left orbit.

"Welcome back, my friend," said Vinson.

"Thanks." McHenry tried to sit up but his hands and feet were bound.

"I'm sorry, Sam," said Dale. "You need to be restrained for the procedure."

He nodded understanding. "That was a neat trick with the fog."

"I didn't know we had it," said Dale. "Adolf thought of it."

Vinson smiled proudly. "Vent heat in the right direction, and a Tiger can even make it rain a little. Coordinate several Tigers underwater and we can change the weather."

"I hadn't yet read that far in the Tiger's manuals."

"You have to be working with these engines for a while. Many things like that are possible. When we return to Berlin, you will see the weather is always perfectly controlled."

"What's happening to Donaldson?"

"It's still morning," said Dale. "He probably just woke up in his bed. Same as his colonel. The memories of the men who were already awake are harder to manage. We didn't have enough time but we did the best we could."

When McHenry didn't react, Dale continued, "That's right. To some extent, we can suppress their memories."

"You can make them forget this happened?"

"Not completely. It's too late for that. The last few hours will be less clear. They will remember but they won't be as certain about it. It will be like memories that are decades old, the way you might remember your early childhood."

"What happens when they compare stories?"

"We'll have to hope it won't matter. We have to make compromises. Any more than that, we damage their minds, and that changes their futures in another way. This isn't perfect by a long shot but it may be enough. We only need that they go on with their lives. You already have people believing crazy things. The war's not even over, and there are people saying that Roosevelt knew Pearl Harbor was going to be attacked. And, naturally, the Jews will say America should have kept fighting this senseless war. A few more Americans with a crazy conspiracy theory won't defeat the Reich downstream."

"*The Jews* again?" prodded McHenry.

"I'm sorry, Sam," she said quietly. It seemed to McHenry that she was reflecting for a moment, genuinely regretful. "It's the way we're brought up. And for that, I am truly sorry."

She paused for only a moment longer, then shifted back, looked into his eyes and said, "This won't hurt."

But it did hurt. It hurt his pride.

His eyes stopped seeing. His ears stopped hearing. His body stopped feeling. He forgot that he ever had arms and legs. He only saw a blank formless image, reminding him of the *Traumsehen* device in *Göring's* infirmary that found the image of the alien ship from his mind. He was awake enough to fear the disclosures that would be ripped from his mind. And he was awake enough to see the image changed by the very fear that he felt.

He never saw anything clearly. But he felt memories of Blanding and Donaldson with him in the Tiger. He remembered wanting to laugh at Blanding's confusion over the presence of women aboard the ship. And he remembered the rifle pointing at him after the initial scuffle with Donaldson. The private's rifle had been pointing at his face, strangely like the feeling when ground gunners were trying to shoot his plane apart, missing the vitals, and then he remembered the bird.

The image changed shape and color, forcing him to break the thought. He felt Blanding's and Donaldson's comfortable presence again. He remembered handing Donaldson the tool from the emergency kit. For a split second, it felt good. That was part of his long-term plan to aid men like Blanding and Donaldson to defeat the Nazis generations hence. Then he remembered where he was, and he wondered how he could have forgotten. He thought again of the ground gunners shooting at him. That was a safe thing to think about. And then he forgot where he was.

*

CHAPTER 22

"Our landings in the Cherbourg-Harve area have failed to gain a satisfactory foothold and I have withdrawn the troops. My decision to attack at this time and place was based upon the best information available. The troops, the air and the Navy did all that bravery and devotion to duty could do. If any blame or fault attaches to the attempt it is mine alone."
— *General Dwight D. Eisenhower,*
(message prepared in the event that D-Day failed)

Wednesday, June 7, 1944

"He is awake."

McHenry recognized Dr. Evers' voice before he opened his eyes. From lighting, and the sterile quality of the air, he knew he was in the infirmary again. When he did look around, he could see Dale and Vinson there, too. "I was expecting you to execute me," he said.

"Almost as bad," said Dale. "We were thinking of keeping you in deep sleep until we return to Berlin."

"How long have I been out?" McHenry looked down, seeing that he was still wearing his Army uniform, but without the jacket. He knew that his mind was clear. He wasn't feeling groggy like the first time he awoke here.

"It has been over two weeks," said the doctor. "This ship is leaving soon. The *Kommandant* thought you should be awake for this. It is our last day over the Earth of your home time."

"Last day?" Feeling frantic, he saw his boots and jacket on another bed beside him. He reached over for the jacket, slipped it on, and checked everything was in place. He vaguely remembered the questionless interrogation session, and avoided looking at the pilot's wings on his uniform. He knew that he'd revealed handing the future technology to Donaldson. He could assume they got it back. But he had tried to forget that he and Donaldson had also exchanged wings.

Had they been able to extract that? he wondered. He dared not think about it now.

"I don't expect to be forgiven," he said. "But I hope you'll understand I did what I needed to do."

"We do understand," said Dale. "We understand duty and honor. I remember telling you, when you first tried to use the escape pod, that we expected you to try. It's in your favor that you didn't do anything stupid."

"Anything stupid?"

"Such as firing on Berlin," said Vinson.

"You're right. I wasn't *that* stupid."

"We know about the device, Sam." said Dale.

He feigned a blank look.

"We know you gave an advanced medical tool to your American comrade. The robots had inventoried the Tiger, and they knew what was missing from the medical kit you stole." She smiled down at him. "It's pretty clever. Setting things up so that the Americans have future technology."

"Yes," agreed Vinson. "They'd lose this war, but might win the cold war that came later after we'd gone. But I am sorry to say that your cleverness will cost you now. Your access throughout the ship may be more restricted when we resume flight operations."

"Resume? You stopped?"

"Like the doctor said," said Dale. "We're pulling out. We have what we need. There's no purpose in continuing to record a history that we want no part of. The next step will be announced after we're safely away in deep space."

"Can I assume that it's past D-Day?" he asked, putting his boots on.

"What are you in such a hurry for?" asked Vinson. "You are not still fighting the war."

"I'd still like to know."

"You just missed it," said Dale. "It's the seventh of June. The Allied commanding general just announced the invasion had failed.

Except for some artifacts of the alternate Grauen, history is mostly progressing as it was expected."

"Meaning?"

"Roosevelt is in hospital. He won't survive the day."

McHenry closed his eyes. The reality hurt, no matter how much he'd known it would happen.

"My condolences," offered the doctor.

"Mine too," added Vinson uncomfortably.

"And mine as well," said Dale. "We know that it is different for you. It might have been better if we had kept you under until we left your time."

"No, I appreciate you all waking me. I need to be up for this." Then, turning, he called, "Rechner, *Spiegel!*" The nearest wall formed a mirror. McHenry looked at the fit of his clothing, which was, of course, still perfect.

Dale smiled, then nodded to Vinson and Dr. Evers. "With primitive garments in the old times, people used mirrors to ensure their clothing was straight."

"It is interesting how quickly he is readjusting back into our world," said the doctor.

"And I still don't need a shave," McHenry mused, feeling his face. He resisted the urge to fidget nervously with his uniform. *The plan might still work out.*

*

"Herr McHenry," addressed the *Kommandant*. She looked down on him, like a teacher addressing a student. "Welcome back to your third chance at life. Do not throw this one away. There will not be a fourth. As this is the Earth of your times, this departure holds special significance for you. I thought it best that you had a view from *Kontrolle*."

"Thank you, ma'am." McHenry stood stiffly, momentarily at attention. Vinson stood beside him and Dale, and then led them to a corner where they could watch the action but stay out of the way.

They were again back in the stationary orbit. The Earth was still majestic, annotated with its grid marks of latitude and longitude, and the markings on the background and foreground. But the view was no longer incomprehensible, having learned what it all meant when he trained to fly the Tiger.

That training was coming in handy now. Although McHenry was not yet proficient in German, he recognized many of the commands and responses as comparable terms used with the Tiger. After a while, he noticed the checklist was visible on a corner of the dome, each item's color changing from red to green as they were counted off. He wondered if he might have a better grasp of what was going on than Dale did, but they stopped at one item he didn't recognize. It was answered by one of the three other SS officers in *Kontrolle*.

"It's about the satellites," Dale whispered. "The SS needs to report a full accounting of satellites. They're still doing an inventory. We couldn't leave if we'd left something behind. Initially, there's the risk that the Grauen could come across one after we leave. Years later, when humanity advances technologically, there's the risk that they'd find one."

One of the SS officers called approval, and the *Kommandant* restarted the countdown, following the checklist. All appeared normal until, a minute later, an operator at one of the sensor stations called an alert.

McHenry stepped closer to Vinson and whispered. "Do you know what's going on?"

"There is something of interest on the surface."

Another crewman came to assist the operator while the *Kommandant* barked orders, and then called to her executive officer.

"We're holding position," Vinson translated.

"Only for a little while," said the *Kommandant*, in English. She then stepped back from the sensor station and looked upward as a tactical map was inset into the dome. McHenry recognized the English Channel. Arrows were pointing to the region on the water.

"There's something unusual about the water," Vinson whispered.

It somehow reminded McHenry of what Vinson had said before they left Hawaii, that a few Tigers would be able to affect the weather. But before he could give it too much thought, new symbols appeared in the area. These were symbols that McHenry knew to mean the Grauen.

He held his breath. Their proximity to the invasion beachhead could only mean the Grauen were interested in the war, after all. Might they be here to turn the war? Is it possible that his own intervention had tipped off the Grauen? Maybe Donaldson and Blanding had something to do with it. He wondered then what Blanding might possibly have done after they left him with the Tiger, even after he had agreed that contacting them would be dangerous — and well above his authority. But it was not to be.

The *Kommandant* barked more orders. Weapons were readied. The number of Grauen increased as they watched the indicator, now understood to be surfacing from underwater. One frame on the left side of the dome showed a Grauen ship doing just that. She spoke again, and the dome center changed modes once more, now showing a close-up view of the ships ascending. There were fifteen of them, grouped together, but not evenly as in a military formation. They appeared to be the old-style Grauen of the type McHenry had seen all those months before. A call out from the sensor section confirmed it. Whatever it was, this was the same generation of Grauen.

The *Kommandant* called out weapons.

"They are planning a cover for Berlin," Vinson whispered. "They are referring to a contingency plan."

They watched as the senior officers deliberated, conferring with the SS officers present, and then with Mtubo and Stern on the screen.

Dale whispered, "The SS is confirming that the war was unaffected. The Grauen had not directly interfered."

The display shifted focus a few times, but it was soon obvious the Grauen were out of the atmosphere, passing deeper into space. They subsequently disappeared, preceded by a tone that McHenry had learned was a field wake alarm, which generally means they're going into interstellar flight. The *Kommandant* said something in German, and the displays went back to normal.

There was another pause as everyone caught their breath.

"Now we all see," said McHenry.

"See what?" Vinson whispered.

"The invasion failed because the Grauen altered the weather. If not for them, Germany would have lost the war." He didn't say it particularly loudly, but from the astonished silence that had permeated the room, he knew that they all had heard.

*

CHAPTER 23

"In South America, it is our mission to make the leadership of Argentina not only possible but indisputable.... Hitler's fight in peace and war will guide us. Alliances will be the next step. We will get Bolivia and Chile. Then it will be easy to exert pressure on Uruguay. These five nations will attract Brazil, due to its type of government and its important group of Germans. Once Brazil has fallen, the South American continent will be ours. Following the German example, we will inculcate the masses with the necessary military spirit."
— *Juan Perón, Vice-President and War Minister of Argentina, (June 10, 1944)*

Saturday, June 10, 1944

"You were right, of course," Dale admitted. They were again in their regular alcove at an SS officers' mess on the fifth-level. The mess was busier this time, but it wasn't crowded.

McHenry looked up at her, not smug, but feeling something of a symbolic victory beside the real defeat. "We would have won the war," he said.

"Perhaps," she said. She looked down at his smaller form, watching him cut the steak. "We can't be certain about Roosevelt's health, of course. The stresses of the defeat would not have been on him. But something else would have gotten to him. He would not have lasted another year."

"But another year is more than enough. And, after a victory across the channel, Wallace would not have given up the war."

"Quite true. And Roosevelt might have lived long enough to begin the next presidential term."

McHenry shook his head. "I don't think he would be running for a fourth term, especially if you say he has health problems."

"If they can hide the fact that he's in a wheelchair, they can hide anything. The system would have run him until he's dead."

He laughed, not taking the bait. "You're always thinking democracy is a cover for conspiracies. You were so sure of your mathematical history but you can't predict whether Roosevelt would have lived through his term."

She laughed, too, but more deviously. "Maybe you've heard the phrase, 'the map is not the territory.' In the sense that we're mapping history, our maps are much, much closer to the territory. They're good — really, really, really good — but they're not one hundred percent. We can only calculate the probability that, had Roosevelt lived, but the invasion still lost, he would still have been compelled to end the war. The English were quite ready to dispose of Churchill. That would have damaged the alliance. But it's less certain." Her expression grew more tense. "And we never considered that the Grauen had plans of their own."

"You know," he mused, "if they keep changing history, there was probably a first version when the Grauen did nothing, and the Allies won the war."

"Don't let that give you solace, Sam. We believe that, whether by happenstance or planning, they've been rewriting our history — probably over and over again. The people of the Reich will never have a real future while they keep meddling. There is only one decisive victory: The last."

"On that last point, at least, we can agree," McHenry said. There was a touch of sadness in his voice.

Dale stirred her spoon in her soup. "You almost had a victory, Sam."

He said nothing to that.

"I mean the medical device that you tried to pass along. It was a clever solution, sacrificing this war for a greater victory in the future, long after we leave."

"I don't see it as that clever at all," he said. "It was the very least thing I could do. I couldn't figure out how to win this war. I couldn't figure out how to save the Jews of Europe. And I couldn't figure out how to save my president. I wasn't nearly clever enough."

"It's not your fault that you're outmatched, Sam. I mean no offense by that. We have some of the finest minds on this ship. We are all genetically enhanced. All the SS personnel here have rechner support implanted into our brains. We have powerful rechners aboard this ship. And when we got the Tiger back, we had very intelligent robots able to quickly search and inventory everything. You got much further in your plot than anyone expected. You did the best that anyone could do. As they used to say in your times, don't sell yourself short."

Someone around a corner had shouted, "*Achtung!*" Hearing a whirl of the clicking of heels, McHenry rose to attention when Dale did. He didn't mind the military formality. He loved it, in fact. But he remembered thinking, those two months ago, that he didn't want to spend the rest of his life heiling the *Führer*. Not Hitler, and not this one. Then quickly, they heard Mtubo telling everyone to sit down until he stood before Dale and McHenry.

"May I join you?" he asked, perfunctorily.

"Certainly, *Oberführer*," Dale replied.

After they sat down, Mtubo, still towering over him, continued what might have been Dale's earlier response. "The Grauen may think they're being benevolent. You do not know the dangers that the future will bring."

"I know what the dangers are today," McHenry replied.

Mtubo shook his head. "We live in a society where any fifteen-year-old may have the knowledge to build a nuclear weapon. Any small group of teenagers has the capacity to create biological weapons that would kill half the people in a city. It takes a well-structured society like ours to control that. By ensuring that national socialism is victorious, the Grauen may have been working to keep humanity from destroying itself."

"You don't think democracies could survive?" McHenry asked, more as a reaction than a question.

"They could not survive without becoming something else. Only nationalist governments — one-party nationalist governments — can impose the politically difficult but critically important policies needed to move a society forward beyond your century."

"Free societies can adapt."

"They will adapt. They will become national socialist." Mtubo relaxed his posture ever-so-slightly, and eased his tone. "Do not misunderstand me, Herr McHenry. I do admire your tenacity. You have inspired me."

"Inspired you?" McHenry was flummoxed. "How?"

"Your plan to have history change after our departure was superior. We had not expected that of you."

"Really?" McHenry's eyes narrowed. "Even had it worked, I thought it was insufficient. I just didn't think there was any other way."

"We are almost at the transit point. We will make an announcement there, but the *Kommandant* has already been informed, and I will tell you now. Our next destination will be the future: an altered future. Our analysts project a national socialist future, and a good one, but not our future. While there we will make a reference survey and then take supplies for a much greater expedition."

A smile was forming on Dale's lips.

Mtubo continued: "And here is the key: My oath, and the oaths of the men and women on this ship, are with our *Führer*, Katrina Renard — not with whomever will be leading the Reich at that future date. After our servicing, we will then be going much further back in time. You see, *Sturmbannführer* Dale has confirmed something in an experiment she conducted." He turned to Dale.

"We can correct the timeline," she said. "Once the Grauen have been removed from our history, we will come back and nudge events back into the sequence we want. It was only a small experiment, but *Göring* can carry it out on a larger scale. We could, potentially, restore the Reich to ninety-eight percent of the way it was when we left."

"Wait a sec," McHenry said. "What do you mean, *removed from history?*"

"Surely, you must have considered this was our goal," said Mtubo, now flashing a smile McHenry had never before seen. "We will eventually be going back further in time, deeper, to a point when the Grauen had not yet evolved. We will end their existence before they end ours."

*

After lunch, McHenry made his way down to the hangar section. *What Mtubo said didn't matter*, he told himself. It was an interesting plan, but he assured himself it would never happen anyway. *Not if they're going to the future first.*

The Tigers were packed and clamped down for interstellar flight. Nevertheless, McHenry was able to climb aboard. If anyone had asked, he'd have said he wanted to reminisce, but no one did. He didn't quite know why, but they had long since accepted his misadventure.

He had two sets of wings on his uniform. One on his "Ike" jacket, and the other on the shirt beneath it. With a flip of one switch, he opened the garbage disposal in the cargo bin. He removed the wings from his shirt, and gave it one quick look. Tossing it from one hand to the other that he might feel the weight, a greater weight came off his shoulders. These were, indeed, the sterling, U.S. Army Air Force issue that he had traded with Donaldson. He placed them into the disposal, and allowed the system to close and cycle, destroying the evidence.

Donaldson had the ones made from a future metal. He wondered how soon he could notice the difference; how long it might take to remember something from his dreams; and then, ultimately, to find what that metal was made from, and exploit that knowledge. That last step may take a couple of generations, he pondered, but that was plenty of time. This war may be lost, but the larger one against a world conquest was not. The United States was going to have one advantage it didn't have before. *Göring* will face a significantly altered future when they arrive. *It should be a free people that fight the Grauen.*

* * * * *

AFTERWORD

When one sees Hitler's December 1943 peace settlement offer (*see Appendix 1*), it's tempting to consider the list and forget the record of the man making those promises. On their face, many of these items would be very crippling to the Third Reich. They suggest that Hitler was willing to go very far. One could easily imagine adding the saving of millions of Jews to the list. But it is doubtful that Hitler would have lived up to such agreements any longer than he considered necessary. This book speculates that he would not.

I've tried to make this book as historically accurate as possible. Epigraph quotes and dates at the start of each chapter are all authentic, and the dates given are as originally printed or when first spoken.

The quotes at the start of chapters 4 and 17 were translations found at the *German Propaganda Archive* by Dr. Randall Bytwerk at Calvin College [www.calvin.edu/academic/cas/gpa/], and used with permission. It's an invaluable resource to get far more than a glimpse of the period.

Although the Tuskegee airmen were real, the characters in this book are not based on anyone in particular. For those who did not know, the Tuskegee airmen were so named because they first trained at the Tuskegee Institute in Alabama. I should not need to explain that 1944 was not the most tolerant time in U.S. history, or any country's history. These men had to put up with the racism of the day, and fight a war besides. But I didn't want this book to be about racism. This is a story about heroism.

It's a valid question whether Nazis could drop the racial elements of their ideology after a number of generations. If they didn't, it's impossible for such a society to be capable of world conquest. At the time, the Nazis themselves were perfectly willing to make alliances with other cultures and races whenever it suited them.

Dale's background explanation for this — while unreliable, and told from a Nazi point-of-view — is mostly true. The Waffen-SS was, indeed, mostly non-German troops. Their stories are not as simple as this, but that is another matter.

Many of Dale's pontifications and distorted history lessons are either based on real history or things the Nazis and their apologists might have said at that time, regardless of whether or not it was factual. As such, everything Dale says in this book needs to be taken with more than a grain of salt. For example, her words calling Germany *"the first country in Europe to overcome the class struggle"* is actually from a quote by Robert Ley, leader of the Nazis' German Labor Front. Because of the war and the Holocaust, people don't usually think of Nazism's social side, but it had a strong one. Dale's phrase "oligarchs of wealth" is actually from Father Charles Coughlin.

I quoted Father Coughlin because his was an American voice of the times, and he is often thought of today as a Nazi apologist. In spite of some critical differences, I do imagine that, had the Nazi ideology ever become dominant worldwide, his influence might have become part of the American blend.

While Dale was obviously lying about the Holocaust, it is true that a small percentage of the victims did die from typhus, notably among them were Anne and Margot Frank.

Although it's certainly true that the Nazis worked restlessly to kill Jews up to the last minute, the largest numbers were killed in 1942 and 1943. McHenry never really had a chance of stopping it, although I do regret myself not being clever enough to write a better attempt.

It was true that there were labor strikes in the U.S. and U.K. during the war, and that this sometimes included strikes at war plants. People today like to think that everyone supported the war effort back then, but that does not mean their support came without bumps in the road. These were sometimes really bad bumps. Yet, as McHenry surmised, those strikes didn't substantively affect supplies for those fighting at the front.

There's no denying that this book was influenced by today's events. Only some of that is intentional. Most references to the peace movement, and Dale's anti-war stance, were with 1944 in mind.

Various elements really were like that. Some did accuse President Roosevelt of waging war for imperialism and for Wall Street.

The U.S. government reacted with congressional hearings of the same type used for communists in the 1930s and — more famously — in the 1950s. The Justice Department put several dozen on trial, as is briefly mentioned in the epigraph at the top of chapter 21.

I know that I've left holes in the backstory. Some would say that Vice President Wallace had communists on his staff who would have pressed him to keep supporting the war while the Soviet Union was in it. To that I say, maybe, but 1944 was an election year. Even those communists would have preferred a Wallace victory to his Republican challenger. And besides, Wallace hated the British Empire. It would have been a more difficult alliance.

Others would argue that the Soviet Union would not have given up after their victories in 1943, even if everyone else did. Dale shrugs this off when McHenry brings it up. In reality, there were several ways this could have worked out, particularly with the Allied bombing campaign out of the picture once the U.S. and the U.K. decided to stand down. The Soviets had not developed that capacity until after the war. I'll agree there must be more to it than that, but this book was focused on Sam McHenry and the United States. And, really, had this book's scenario actually occurred, you could expect the Grauen to have surreptitiously aided Germany on the Eastern Front just as they had in Normandy.

— R.M.B.

APPENDIX 1

Reported Peace Settlement Offer of December 1943

1. Eventual evacuation by Germany of all occupied and conquered territory, including Czechoslovakia.

2. Abandonment of all German claims to colonies.

3. Ultimate disestablishment of the German navy.

4. Germany to retain no merchant navy as such but to reach an agreement with Britain regarding German overseas shipments.

5. Abolition of Nazi propaganda abroad.

6. An agreement with the Allies on civil aviation.

7. Germany ultimately to cease maintenance of an air force.

8. Germany to remain always in close consultation with Britain on matters concerning common defense interests.

Source: *Associated Press, (April 17, 1944)*

Note: This peace offer was not extended to the Soviet Union.

*

APPENDIX 2

Table of SS, Luftwaffe and U.S. Army ranks in 1944

SS	Luftwaffe	U.S. Army
Officer ranks		
Reichsführer-SS[1]	Generalfeldmarschall	General of the Army[2]
Oberstgruppenführer	Generaloberst	General
Obergruppenführer	General	Lieutenant General
Gruppenführer	Generalleutnant	Major General
Brigadeführer	Generalmajor	Brigadier General
Oberführer	(none)	(none)
Standartenführer	Oberst	Colonel
Obersturmbannführer	Oberstleutnant	Lieutenant Colonel
Sturmbannführer	Major	Major

Hauptsturmführer	Hauptmann	Captain
Obersturmführer	Oberleutnant	First Lieutenant
Untersturmführer	Leutnant	Second Lieutenant
NCO ranks		
Sturmscharführer (Waffen-SS only)	Stabsfeldwebel	Sergeant Major
Hauptscharführer	Oberfeldwebel	Master Sergeant
Oberscharführer	Feldwebel	Sergeant First Class
Scharführer	Unterfeldwebel	Staff Sergeant
Unterscharführer	Unteroffizier	Sergeant
Enlisted ranks		
Rottenführer	Obergefreiter	Corporal
Sturmmann	Gefreiter	Private First Class
Obermann Oberschütze (Waffen-SS)[3]	Obersoldat[3]	(none)

Mann Schütze (Waffen-SS)	Flieger	Private
Anwärter (Candidate)	(none)	(none)
Bewerber	(none)	(none)

1. Reichsführer-SS was both an office and a rank held by only one person at a time. Heinrich Himmler held this post from 1929 to 1945.
2. The rank of General of the Army, as a five-star general, was not created until December 14, 1944 by act of Congress.
3. Oberschütze and Obersoldat were specialist ranks used by the Heer (Army) and ground forces of the Luftwaffe. It was divided into specialties, *Oberkanonier, Obergrenadier, Oberpionier, Oberfahrer* and *Oberfunker.* In the real world, this level was abolished when ranks were standardized with NATO.

26618870R00117

Made in the USA
Lexington, KY
09 October 2013